DROP YOUR TOXIC PAST

RITA MCGLOTHIN

Printed in the United States of America

First Printing, 2024

Just Be Beautiful Incorporated Publishing

285 W. Wieuca Rd NE

PMB 4387

Atlanta, Georgia 30342

United States

www.justbebeautiful.org

ISBN: 979-8-9903328-0-5

CONTENTS

BEFORE YOU GET STARTED...
REFERENCE WORDS. TOOLS.

Here are a few words that are used throughout this life-changing book:

Word	Definition
Toxic	Extremely harsh, malicious, & harmful; capable of causing death or debilitation; **
Toxicity	The quality or state being poisonous;**
Reject	To refuse; disown;*
Rejection	To disallow; to refuse to consider; to disavow or disclaim;**
Rejected	Fail to show due affection or concern; to dismiss as inadequate;*
Past	Just gone, elapsed; having existed or taken place in a period before the present**

*Thomas Nelson Publishers (1982). In *Three-in-one concise Bible reference companion.* (pp. 575-576). Nashville.

**Merriam-Webster. (n.d.). Toxicity. In *Merriam-Webster.com dictionary*. Retrieved August 22, 2020, from https://www.merriam-webster.com/dictionary/toxicity

**Merriam-Webster. (n.d.). Toxic. In *Merriam-Webster.com dictionary*. Retrieved August 22, 2020, from https://www.merriam-webster.com/dictionary/toxic

**Merriam-Webster. (n.d.). Rejection. In *Merriam-Webster.com dictionary*. Retrieved August 22, 2020, from https://www.merriam-webster.com/dictionary/rejection

**Merriam-Webster. (n.d.). Past. In *Merriam-Webster.com dictionary*. Retrieved August 23, 2020, from https://www.merriam-webster.com/dictionary/past

INTRODUCTION

This book is for anyone who has a past. This book is for anyone who is living in regret about a past mistake or simply their overall past. Are you holding on to the past like a vice grip? Well, this book is for you and anyone who had a past and no longer claims it as theirs (That's me!). This book is for anyone who is currently rejecting their past and no longer desires its existence. This book is for anyone who wants to deem their circumstance and PRESENT negative situation officially *THE PAST*. Yes, you guessed it! This book is for **YOU**!

Everyone has a past, but your past does not have to grip you, HOLD you, take control of you, or lead you. Your past must pledge allegiance to your present and your future. You have the power to make your past come under subjection and surrender to your control and command. Why? You cannot do anything to change what happened, those things are gone. It HAPPENED. You cannot change the past, however, you CAN change your perspective and how you live out your present situation into your future.

I am a BELIEVER, a Woman of God. I believe that God

protects my present life from the effects of my past mistakes and blunders. Therefore, I believe that my past has been thrown into the Sea of Forgetfulness (Micah 7:18-20; Romans 8:1) and annihilated from existence. It would be so silly of me to jump into the sea and try to retrieve it. It is gone! I believe that if others attempt to awaken my past or bring it up again, I will not accept it nor will it negatively affect me. Why? It no longer controls me. It does not have a place in my life. I tell **IT** when **IT** can come out and under what conditions and criteria for doing so. I put my past under subjection to the Word of God, which is the incorruptible seed. I have turned my past into a learning tool. It was only there to show me how far I have grown from the foolish mistakes I made.

Goodbye!

It's time to say 'goodbye' to the effects of your past. It has been holding you back for so long. Stop holding on to the rope of 'tug o' war' because it is stopping you from progressing. You can't go forward because the past keeps you bound and pulls you back to opening old wounds, cuts, scars, and bruises. Let them heal or you will live in regret, just as I did. I allowed my past mistakes and bad relationships to creep into my present life, potential money relationships, personal relationships, profession, as well as business relationships— only to look up and see my relationships utterly destroyed. Why? *THAT DAMNED PAST!! I had to tell the past to *GO TO HELL! Because that's where it belongs, today! Here is one of my favorite Biblical scriptures that keeps me moving forward, **Philippians 3:13: "13 No, dear brothers and sisters, I have not achieved it,[a] but I focus on this one thing: Forgetting the past and looking forward to what lies ahead,...**

You don't have to share your past in detail to help someone, to achieve credibility with them, or even for someone to listen to you. So, come along with me as I share how you can break free from THAT HELL-BOUND PAST. It's time for you to enjoy life the way God designed it for you: living your best life without bones, scraps, skeletons, or bodies in your closet. Let's clean the closet out and burn the old, distressful memories. Allow me to show you how to DROP YOUR TOXIC PAST.

P.S. This is a clarifying statement for my readers. I can use 'DAMN' & 'HELL' because they are in The Bible and I am using them in the proper context.

1

THE PARENT PAST

MOM. DAD. GRANDS. FOSTER. STEPPARENTS.

We cannot pick our parents. We cannot rewrite how *our parents* were raised. We cannot rewrite how we were raised; and unfortunately, we had no control over how they treated us when we were living in their homes and under their care. Mothers, Fathers, Grandparents, Foster parents, Stepparents, or Godparents are our first teachers. These are people who we typically look up to for guidance, mentorship, care, love, trust, to supply answers to questions, and some of our basic needs. However, there are times where we receive bad teachings from them that may be confusing. Additionally, life happens and our parents or caregivers may make a direct or indirect decision that hurts us. Here's one of a few examples that I will share in this Parent Past chapter.

Throughout my life, I've had many people to cross my path as friends. Some made an indelible mark on my life, and some did not—to the point where I don't even remember them. However, I remember this one girl who befriended me in high school. She was academically strong, very few friends, tall, stately and a great basketball player. Let's call her Ann.

Scenario: *Ann*

Ann and I became friends because we shared an interest in Math, Science, and good books. One day, Ann invited me to her house to work on a school project. When I arrived at her house, I was in total amazement. Her home was huge! It was a tall brick house with a large porch and beautiful land-scaping. I thought to myself,"Wow!" "Ann's parents must be rich!"

I walk into the foyer, passing the formal dining room and into the large living room. My mouth is open with constant compliments to Ann, "You have a beautiful home." "This is nice." Ann modestly says, "Thanks." So, she introduces me to her grandmother, then whisks me off upstairs to her bedroom. We sit down on the floor, pull out our project papers, and begin to work. Suddenly, I ask Ann, "where's your Mom?" "Don't you have to ask for permission to have company?" She replies, "It's fine my grandmother takes care of me." So, I asked another question, "Where's your dad?" Ann's body language tells me that she is slightly uncomfortable, a little sad, yet ready to reveal something to me. Suddenly, she sits back and explains in a low tone that her father is in the military, and her mother is deceased.

Kids are curious, yet compassionate. Being that nosey and empathetic kid, I asked Ann, "What happened to your Mom?" She explains that she lived in Seattle with her parents. Her mother had an assistant position in a dental office. One evening, her mother and another co-worker were assigned to clean the office and lock up. So Ann's mom and the intern/friend decided to 'get high' by breathing in little puffs of the "laughing gas" or anesthesia. Unfortunately, they experienced a bad reaction to the gas. They were found dead on the dental office floor.

My heart dropped and one little tear rolled down my face. I sat back and just stared at Ann. I could not imagine losing my mother, especially in that way and during my teenage years. My empathy level increased for Ann. I tried to process her life as my own, thinking about not having a mother and a dad being in the military. She was missing both parental nurturing. Now, I understood why she was slightly reclusive, quiet, and had minimal friends. "How can I help my friend, Ann?"

As you can see, I never forgot about Ann. After thirty-one years, I still remember that story, the images in my head of when she told me what happened to her mom and how Ann's face looked when she told me. However, the most interesting thing about this whole encounter was that Ann did not cry, nor was she sad as she reflected on the details. She was sort of numb or unmoved by it all. She changed the subject and we moved on to complete our project.

THE VISIBLE WOUNDS: *Roots of Rejection*

- Death of one or both parents. Extended separation from the father or paternal spirit
- No Maternal or Mother-guidance. She has a Mother's Love deficit.
- Hardness | nonchalant or a "I-don't-care" attitude. Pushing away people
- Self-sabotaging behavior or destroying relationships before they start

- Being a Loner or not having many friends.
  Refusing to get close to anyone [family, friends]

The above list is not an all-inclusive, exhaustive list. There may be other signs, symptoms, red flags, or issues one may see in someone like Ann. However, if these wounds go unchecked or unresolved, they will remain open, become infected, and go down to the bone of a person. This is what I describe as "The Root of Rejection" or "ROR." It takes much longer and more time to uproot the Roots of Rejection than healing a wound of rejection. ROR's have a habit of popping up at the best times of one's life. They rear their ugly heads and begin to infect other people who come into the rejected person's life.

Let's see how unresolved wounds (The Past) affected Ann's life as an adult woman with children: *(this account is derived from spending time with Ann, after bumping into her at an event a few years ago.)*

- She is now a successful IT Engineer for a government agency, with a very small team. She prefers to work alone, however, her boss requires that she build and mentor teammates.
- Ann debates with her colleagues and teammates quite often because she feels that she is right or the most sensible one in the group.
- She is a divorced mother of two children; one boy & one girl.
- Her relationship with both children is acceptable, but could be better. She is harder on her daughter than she is with her son.
- Ann is "mad at God" for the life she feels like she was dealt while growing up. Therefore, her

connection to people, who are spiritual, is uncomfortable and distant.

- She can sometimes present herself as angry or bitter. She over-talks everyone in the conversation, including men. She thrives on being controlling.
- Ann repels women. In fact, she has expressed in the past conversations that she prefers to have more male friends and associates than women. She explains that she does not trust women.

THE VISIBLE SCARS: *Healing Process.*

As you can see, Ann's *Parent-Past* affected her present circumstances and possibly her long-term future goals. However, all is not lost. Healing is available for Ann if she wants it. Let me say that again, "Healing is available for Ann if she wants it."

The key to the breakthrough for her healing process is:

1. **Ann must recognize that she needs healing for her emotions and thinking.** She must see it for herself or someone must show that her emotions are damaged and out of place. Ann must be taught and shown that her mindset and thinking are warped and unhealthy. She must see that her emotions, thinking, and behavior are destroying potentially great connections, as well as opportunities.

2. **Ann must desire to be healed and changed; as well as pursue them.** This means that she has finally reached a point in her life where she is

tired of going through vicious cycles, getting the same negative results, and experiencing feelings of defeat. Ann must begin to research and reflect on how she arrived at this point in her life. She may have arrived at this point because someone commented on her behavior, her kids may have said something to her or she recognized that she has been hindered from reaching a certain goal. Once she identifies the *Root Cause* behind the damaged emotions, then her warped thinking and negative behavior must be uprooted. (Possibly with the help of a therapist, counselor or clergy member)

3. **Ann must begin the Process of Uprooting Roots and Healing Open Wounds.** She will begin to create a My Life Timeline© of events, starting at her childhood—as early as she can remember. The My Life's Timeline© template is located in the Reference Pages of this book. The timeline will take Ann through a time capsule of how her life began or the first memories, whether good or bad. It will serve as a visual image to show her exactly 'what went wrong' and 'when it went wrong.' The timeline will propel Ann to begin asking herself questions similar to these:

4. Why am I so distant with people, especially women? Why do I have more men in my life, as friends and colleagues than women?

5. Why do I have to control every situation?

6. Why do I over-talk people when having a conversation?

7. Why am I always alone and never cultivating a healthy romantic relationship?
8. Ann will dig deep by asking herself, "Why did I get a divorce? What was my part in the divorce?
9. Why is my relationship with my daughter different from my mother-son relationship?
10. **Once Ann begins the process, she must be consistent. Ann cannot stop until the healing process is complete.** This is what the on-going healing process looks and sounds like if Ann truly wants to heal. This is what it may sound like if she had an Accountability Partner, a therapist or a counselor:

- It's time to forgive Mom for suddenly leaving you when you were only a teenager.
- It's time to stop comparing your father to your friends' fathers. It's time to release your father from any expectations that you had outside of the care he provided while serving in the military.
- It's time to forgive yourself for all of the hurt and pain that you inflicted physically and mentally on yourself and your kids.
- It's time to ask your kids for forgiveness and to apologize to them. Additionally, it's time to secure a Family Counselor so that everyone is going through a healing process. This will ensure that the Roots of Rejection are not passed on to the next generation.
- It's time to forgive yourself for sabotaging great relationships. (If you are a Believer, rest assured that God gives us second chances.)

- (If you are a Believer) It's time to ask God to forgive you for all of the direct and indirect hurt inflicted on your colleagues, women, and men— who only wanted to be your friend.
- It's time to allow God back into your heart and see Him as Love, Peace & Comfort.

5. **Surround yourself with Positive Productive People.** When surrounding yourself with positive people, ensure that these positive people are going where you want to go or have arrived at where you are trying to go. Also, be careful not to get comfortable with reminiscing over the past and "Swapping War Stories" with people in your circle.

6. **The past has passed. It's over and gone, so start fresh.** Continue to move forward and not fall into a trap of regret. Don't beat yourself up about past mistakes. Everyone has made mistakes, but some did not recover from them. You recovered! So, give yourself a chance to prove to yourself that you can get it right the next time around. Drop Your Toxic Past!

OTHER PARENT-PAST SCENARIOS

You may not be able to relate to Ann's situation because you experienced something totally different from your parents. You may have had both parents in the home, providing for you and your other siblings, but never spending time with you. Or you may be able to identify with some of these Parent-Past situations:

- *BROKEN FAMILY SCENARIO:* Father is extremely abusive to you, your siblings, and your mother. He abruptly leaves the home when you were in Kindergarten. Your Mom decides to uproot the entire family and move you all to another region of the country. She meets a very stable, nice gentleman, remarries and he adopts you and your siblings. As you mature into your early teens, you begin to show signs of the 'Abandonment Syndrome' with friends and family. This is where you reject yourself before someone else rejects you. This is where you only allow a small, handful of people in your life. This is where you become reclusive and standoff-ish to everyone, including your parents.

- *Why? Here it is*: Mom never sat down with a family counselor, a therapist, or any type of Domestic Violence Hotline Help* Experts to properly heal. She was afraid for her life and family, so she ran as fast as she could run and as far as she could go. Mom never explained to you and your siblings what happened between her and your father. You often ask yourself questions of Why did he leave us? Why does he not love us? Where is he now? Will I ever see him again?

- *CAUTION:* If you are asking these questions, it is time to heal by asking for help. It is time that your past no longer haunts you. If you continue to allow the past to haunt you, it will rob you of quality relationships. You will push away quality people who have crossed your path for a reason. It's time for you to Drop Your Toxic Past before the toxicity destroys your future relationships.

*National Domestic Violence Hotline: 1-800-799-7233 | 1-

800-787-3224 (TTY) or online at https://www.thehotline.org/ OR Text **LOVEIS** to 22522

- *SIBLING SCENARIO:* It's just you and your younger sister. You and your sister are one-year apart. Mom and Dad are in the home and the entire family is active, as well as athletic. Your entire family enjoys coming together and having family celebrations, fun gatherings, as well as commemorative events. It all seems so warm and loving, but there's this one thing that keeps bothering you. Every time the family is together, or Mom takes you and your sister out somewhere, she loves to compare you to your younger sister. She always says so boisterously to the crowd, "Well, you know they are like night and day!" Of course, you know who "night" is... YOU. Your Mom follows this up with, "Girl, why can't you be like your sister? She behaves nicely." This statement angers you and makes you feel devalued and inadequate. It makes you resent your younger sister. Sometimes you feel like slapping her or playing a really mean practical joke on her.
- *Why? Here it is:* Mom does not realize that words and phrases, passed along from generation to generation, can really hurt someone. We are all born with our own set of emotions and unique wiring. Everyone does not have 'thick skin' or can just let it 'roll off their backs.' Mom and Dad may have been taught to be tough or given the same labels that they currently use. Therefore, they continue to

unconsciously perpetuate the hurt onto their children.

- *CAUTION:* If you don't heal the wounds from these hurting words, then you will continue this vicious cycle for another twenty years. The relationship between you and your sister may become strained for no fault of hers. Inflicted hurt on your younger sister will cause her to walk around with a wound, as well. So, you have to ask your Mom to stop comparing you to your sister. Ask your Mom and Dad to see your talents. Forgive your Mom and Drop Your Toxic Past.

- *FATHER SCENARIO:* You grew up without the love and guidance of a father. You lacked the father-figure in the home like many other men and women in this world. You are not alone. He met your mother during a rough time in her life. He came to provide some normalcy, comfort, and peace. Then, you came along, born into an unwed, non-committed relationship. Everything went well for about four years and then— NOTHING! He disappears into thin air, at least that's what your four-year-old brain processes. This action was your first let-down. It happened that day when you waited for him to pick you up to take you to your cousin's birthday party, but he never showed up. You waited by the side kitchen doorway for hours and he never showed up. So, you turn to your Mom and asks, "Where is my Dad?" "I thought that he was coming to pick me up?" Your mother replies, "He's not coming." She storms out of the room and leaves you standing there so confused. You weep. Later, you discover that he is gone for life. You will probably never see him again. It has been revealed that if you see him again, it will be when you are an adult. So, you pray that you will get the chance to ask him what happened and to hug his neck. Well, low and behold, your prayers are answered. He reappears when you are an adult who is following your dreams and passion for life. You set up a meeting with him to catch up and start anew. He tells you that life for him is different, he has a new family, and basically "Right now, you don't fit." Second major let-down—you are crushed and utterly disappointed. Now, your heart is hardened to where you decide to sever the ties between child and father.

- **Why? Here it is:** Your father is just THAT: a man who fathered you to be in the world. He did not plan for you to be here. Furthermore, he had no deep connection with your mother. Your father cannot give you what he does not have. He cannot love you because he does not have *Love* to give. He cannot be a loving dad because he grew up without life lessons on how to be a loving dad. He was a young boy who fathered a child. The single, street life was all he knew. The single, street life was what he knew how to nurture, love, and embrace; not a child. You are expecting him to be something that he did not sign up for and never knew how to execute.

- **Caution:** If you continue to hold on to the hurt, unhealed wounds, and the painful let-downs of your father, you will possibly hate men, distrust men, nor allow many men in your life, even as friends. Hurt distorts your view of yourself and others: meaning how you see things from that moment and into the future. Hurt keeps you stuck in the past and prevents you from going forward. It has a dangerous possibility for your life: it makes you bitter towards yourself and others. Forgiveness is first. Forgive him for his ignorance or not knowing, as well as the lack of desire to know fatherhood. Also, you must release the expectations of your father. You are expecting to get something from him that he does not possess and cannot retrieve. It's the same as if you are expecting an apple tree to produce oranges. It's not there. Do yourself a huge, beneficial favor: release him once and for all, forgive him, treat yourself with love and care. Please open your heart to mentorship from a true father-figure. You may be able to find fatherly guidance from positive Men's Group or Ministry, your local church, an intramural community sports group, or an online relationship coach. Let's break the cycle. Let's Drop the Toxic Past.

2

THE STD, STI & SEX PAST

SEXUALLY TRANSMITTED DISEASES.
SEXUALLY TRANSMITTED INFECTIONS.
SEXUAL ENCOUNTERS.

Of course, I had to include these two topics in the book: Sex and STDs. I consider Sex and STD/STI topics the second and third most important issues, behind the Parent Past, that plague a person's progress and future relationships. You would be surprised by how many people, including beautiful, upstanding good girls and handsome, put-together, "swagged-out", good guys are carrying the First-Time Sex encounter and possibly the STD past in their heart. I've read about it, heard about it, met others, and chatted with people who revealed the infections they were carrying. They have also shared the experiences with me, while seeking treatment, along with hiding from the stigma attached to these diseases. Unfortunately, some of these people deal with another wound: the horrible first-time, losing their virginity experience, which still haunts them. It haunts them in such a way that they lose sleep, friends, and opportunities because of it. Many of these precious people have missed out on great relationships because they became reclusive and pulled away from people due to the first-time sex issue.

Others have hidden in the shadows because of the stigma attached to having had or currently carrying an STD—from that first sex encounter.

My heart goes out to these precious people because society has truly ostracized honest, good people with STD's. (*Side Note: I have to make this distinction because there are people out in this world who knowingly have an STD/STI, do not disclose it, and purposely infect as many people as they can infect. The statistical data says that there are 20 million people in the United States or in other words, 1 out of 6 people who have been diagnosed with HSV 1, HSV 2, or both infections. Additionally, there are HSV 2 carriers who are not aware they are carrying the infection. However, when they find out the diagnosis, they feel ashamed or embarrassed.*) So, society makes them feel weird, dirty, and shameful. They feel isolated and alone. They feel like life, especially their love life, is over completely and forever!

One Sunday morning, I remember listening to a pastor preach a sermon on "You Are Not Your Past. So Move On." At first, I got super bothered by this title. I thought to myself, "Boy, Oh boy! This is so insensitive!" I thought about those precious people carrying the guilt and shame of losing their virginity and possibly living with STD's. I said to myself, "Actually, they are their past because they have to tell their future partner about what happened or what they've contracted. And guess what, insensitive Pastor? They may have to deal with being rejected by someone who they truly like and care about." In my head, I continued to rebuttal the Pastor's sermon with various topics like abortion, rape, physical & permanent scars from domestic violence, PTSD, and many other traumatic past scenarios. Well, it seemed as if the Pastor could hear my thoughts because every time I thought one thing, he had an answer and scripture for it.

"DANG! This guy is good." That's when God spoke through that Pastor, directly to me, and said, "People have to stop crowning themselves as 'the god' over their situation. Let God handle it." This was a true eye-opener. I said to myself, "Wow, THAT'S IT!!" This meant the following to me: if you are dealing with a physical scar from your past, including an existing STD or STI, of course, get treated and take care of yourself. However, while you are doing the common sense things, Let God choose and set your path for great relationships. Don't shut yourself off from the world, then become a nun or a priest, take a vow of celibacy, and push away people. However, I would recommend abstaining from any sexual relationships until marriage. While you abstain from sex, I recommend getting educated about your health. Research ways on how to heal emotionally and physically from the effects of rape, molestation, losing your virginity, and/or contracting an STD or STI. Additionally, get educated on how to have a conversation with your future partner about these effects and possible triggers. Watch videos and read articles that the Centers for Disease Control and Prevention (CDC)* has produced. There are even brave people who have started blogs and private support groups for these situations. Remember, you are not alone. You will be surprised by the acceptance and embrace you will receive through your willingness to be transparent and honest with yourself.

SCENARIO: *Luke*

Luke was 'reborn' into a two-parent household. At two years old, he had been placed up for adoption. In no time, a loving couple adopted Luke and raised him as their very own. He was loved unconditionally by his mother but given strict, tough love by his father. Luke's father provided for the family by working long, hard hours throughout the week. Based on Luke's perception, his father did not spend true quality time with him. Coaching sports and talking to Luke about life and growing into a man was what his father enjoyed doing most. Years went by and Luke enters college. He joins several college committees and male groups to forge a bond with other like-minded guys. Luke was also craving a brotherhood and that long-lost sibling connection. Remember, he grew up the only child, with the "adopted stamp" in his heart. So there was always a void in his heart for his biological parents, as well as siblings. Well, one day, Luke's college life took a turn for the 'even-better.' He met Sheila, Andy, Sharon, Trudy, Bethany, Deanna, and many more college women. Luke had become popular with the ladies since he joined the male groups on campus. His attractiveness and intellect became extremely appealing to the masses. He thought to himself, "Wow! I can get used to this." So, he shared this newfound fame with some of his college friends and roommates. They celebrate with Luke by giving him the 'Bro-hug' or fist-bump or high-five or Bro-shove. Then, one of the upper-class brothers tells him to love them all. He encourages Luke to not just choose one. He mentors Luke on how to juggle at least three at one given time. So he went for it. Luke started going out with two and three college ladies at-a-time. He took his friends' advice and remembered to date women whose paths rarely crossed. He made sure that they did not stay in the same dorms or campus apartments. He even tried not to date women who were in the same Academic Major, but it was difficult because they were all so lovely. Luke did not discriminate when it came to their age. He dated freshmen and upperclassmen, alike. These encounters gave him his first experiences of fabulous, exhausting sex. He could not contain himself. It was all so fulfilling, so strengthening, so powerful, and so ego-boosting.

Fast-forward to college graduation, where Luke is a Mathematics degree grad with honors. He is still popular with the ladies, but he meets Jillian. She is gorgeous, adventurous, and ready to see the world. Jillian and Luke talk for hours after graduation until they decide to call it a night or 'morning.' They decide to meet one another the next evening before College Move-Out day. Jillian and Luke meet at the coffee shop. Suddenly, they lock eyes, hug, kiss, and decide to go back to her apartment. That night was pure ecstasy. There was nothing in the world that mattered to them as they had multiple sexual experiences until sunrise.

College Move-Out day is here, everyone is saying their 'good-byes' and 'see-you-soon' throughout the campus. Luke and Jillian chat over the phone and make plans to stay in touch. They depart for the airport and set off to begin their careers as new college grads. For two months, they stay in touch by phone, pager, letters, and a few quick flights for a weekend visit to one another's resident city. Then, during one of those in-person visits, Jillian breaks the news to Luke that he is going to be a dad. This is not what he wanted to hear. He was sorely disappointed and left her residence upset. Luke calls his parents, tells them the news, and listened to his parent's advice, "Stick with her and raise your child." He tries to do this but the relationship is strained, Jillian's family gets involved and turns them against each other.

Fifteen years go by, Luke has no quality relationship with his teenage daughter or mother of his child. Unfortunately, he has not visited them in years. He has no desire to forge a strong relationship with anyone in either family, especially now that his mother is deceased. He is discouraged, so he continues to throw himself into his first loves... Math & Money. Luke is a successful budget analyst, has his side hustle, owns real estate, has no desire to be married, and dates multiple beautiful women throughout the country. The only problem is that the relationships are short-lived. Even when Luke thinks that he has found a woman with whom he can have a long-term relationship, it comes to a terrible end. Either he has to get a restraining order on the woman, change his number or she dumps him because of his non-stop, warped demands for sexual adventures and experiences.

WHY? **Here it is:**

- Abandonment by one or both parents: He never resolved why his parents gave him up for adoption. He is still living with the void and trying to fill the void with everything else.
- Luke wants to fill the void by having people around him. Growing up without siblings, being rejected by his biological parents, and given tough love by his adopted father area all infected wounds of rejection.
- Luke uses sex as a pacifier for loneliness and to fill the hole that rejection has caused.
- He lacks a mentor and a true male connection with someone who will love him no matter the circumstances and mistakes.
- Luke unconsciously chooses and attracts broken women because of his college lessons and promiscuity. He knows that these women have a

need to feel loved or a sense of belonging just as he does. So two broken, unhealed people come together to try and build a fantasy relationship. It ends in more hurt.

- Luke is unconsciously perpetuating the cycle of rejection and abandonment with his daughter. He was not ready to be a father.

CAUTION: If he does not heal, then Luke will end up being the main character of a tragic love triangle story. He may end up living life, never married, never healed, and adding deeper wounds to broken women's lives. He may end up contracting an STD or HIV, unknowingly infecting someone else and destroying their life, along with his life.

Or, he will meet an amazing woman who has her life in order and wants to be in a relationship. But because Luke is broken, has a warped view about sex, and loves booty calls, he will push this amazing woman away...ultimately missing out on a great relationship and maybe the answer to his prayers. Luke needs a male mentor who can provide him with guidance to get therapy for his adoption voids, his sexual promiscuity, and his estranged relationship with his daughter. It's time for Luke to Drop his Toxic Past so that he can live a healthy fulfilling, authentic life.

SCENARIO: *Delilah*

She is a beautiful Jamaican born and raised 25-year old woman, who is out-going, athletic, and loves fashion. Her name is Delilah and she is such a cheerful young lady. However, Delilah hides something deep behind her smile and ambition, the hurt and rejection experienced at the hands of her three older sisters. They treated her so badly while growing up because they were jealous of her beauty. They believed that she was treated better by their parents and the neighborhood families because of her natural beauty and talent. This ill-treatment created a strain between Delilah and her three sisters. It made her so uncomfortable to the point where she hated to attend family gatherings. It was at the family gatherings, the sisters would arrive with insults and sarcastic remarks. All Delilah wanted was to be loved and accepted by the ones closest to her. This deeply hurt her and she wanted a way of escape.

Well, the day came where Delilah could truly escape. A dear friend submitted some of Delilah's photos to an athletic and fitness company for a modeling opportunity. The company fell in love with Delilah's photos and presented her with the opportunity of a lifetime. Arrangements were made and she relocated to America to pursue a career in the athletic-fitness industry. It did not take long for Delilah to make friends, make money, and make heads turn. She was a natural beauty, sweet and kind, but a true go-getter. It is safe to say that she was super popular with everyone, especially with her new love interest. Delilah was finally feeling the love and acceptance that she missed receiving back home in Jamaica.

It was a beautiful Miami Beach sunset. Delilah and her new guy, Sam, decided to go for an evening stroll along the beach. They held hands, laughed, talked, and stopped to kick sand on one another's ankles for fun. There was no doubt that there was chemistry between them, so things started to get a little hot along the beach stroll. Sam grabbed Delilah from behind and pressed his body against hers, allowing her to feel his nature rising. He whispered in her ear that he had fallen for her and that she was the most beautiful woman he had ever loved. They kissed. Delilah liked the kiss but felt slightly uncomfortable because she was still a virgin. Sam guided her back to his convertible so that they could make a quick drive to his condo. When they arrived, Sam wined and dined Delilah with his favorite wine and hors d'oeuvres. They laughed, kissed, and held each other close. Delilah wanted so badly to pull away and tell him about her virginity but she did not want to push him away. He was everything she ever wanted in a man, including his seven-year age difference. She had a 'thing' for older men. Things started to get so steamy that Sam removed his shirt, then attempted to remove Delilah's clothes. She stopped him by quickly blurting out, "We can't do this! I'm a virgin." Sam insists that he would be gentle because he had fallen in love with her. Delilah relaxed her body and allowed Sam to be "her first."

One week had passed, the relationship between Sam and Delilah had grown intimately closer, and business was booming for both of them. They continued to spend time talking during her photo shoots and his executive meetings. At the week's end, Delilah began to feel a little like she was catching a cold. Her throat was scratchy, she had the worst headache ever, and her chilly body ached. Friday morning Delilah took a day off from work because the symptoms had gotten worse. She was now feeling a burning sensation in her pelvic area and vagina. "What is going on?" She thought to herself. Delilah rushes out to visit an urgent care clinic and gets the most devastating diagnosis ever: Herpes Simplex 2 (HSV-2). All of her cold-like symptoms were a byproduct of contracting HSV-2. Delilah silently wept in the doctor's office for at least fifteen minutes. She could not believe it; she had HSV-2 in which there is no cure. "Oh, my

God! I will carry this forever. My life is over!" The doctor attempted to comfort her in the most compassionate, yet professional way. The doctor told her to pull herself together because she had one main thing to do when she leaves the office: *Tell your partner*.

Before breaking the news to Sam, Delilah decides to call her bestie, Naomi. Naomi cried with Delilah and told her not to trust this guy. She prepped Delilah to listen for the lies and denial that come along with sleaze bags like Sam. Naomi urged Delilah to break up with him, cut her losses on letting him be her first, and move on by focusing solely on her career. So, that evening, Delilah breaks the news to Sam; and to her surprise, he did not know that he even had HSV-2. The virus lies dormant in some people's bodies, as it had for Sam. He rushes out to an urgent clinic to get tested and the results are positive. Delilah goes against her friend's advice and remains with Sam; because she believed him one hundred percent. She loved him with all of her heart and soul.

Unfortunately, Sam and Delilah's relationship began to crumble after a month of finding out the news. Sam began to pull away because he felt a bit of remorse for unknowingly infecting Delilah and hiding his girlfriend of two years. Yes, there was someone else—the other woman—from whom he had contracted HSV-2. The Other Woman had never left Sam's side, nor his condo. She was just out of the country visiting family and friends. Upon her return, he confronted the Other Woman, but decided to stay with her and totally drop Delilah. He had invested two years into the Other Woman, and figured that Delilah was young and can bounce back. Poor Delilah...devastated, heart-broken, living in total regret and depressed.

. . .

WHY? Here it is:

- Rejection pushed her into the arms of a slick thief and con-artist. He convinced her that her morals, boundaries and standards would be safe with him.
- Delilah trusted him because he was older and seemingly wiser.
- Delilah had voids or holes within her that had never been filled with healthy emotions and the right perspective about acceptance. So she made a bad decision of allowing her void to be filled with a temporary fix: affection and sex.
- Her past Family Rejection was painful and hurt to the core of her being. She never fully healed from these wounds, therefore she allowed her successful career to disguise itself as the cure.
- She did not recognize her value and worth. Even though she was complimented on her natural beauty, ambition and athleticism, it wasn't a foundation on which she could build a strong sense of self worth.
- She gave up her most prized possession, her precious body and virginity. She naively turned it over to someone who did not care about her priceless value and worth. She turned it over to a selfish, deceptive person with cheap motives.

CAUTION: If she does not heal, then Delilah will travel down a road of darkness, terminal regret, and ultimately— tragedy. Oftentimes, people who have experienced the type of multi-level rejection such as Delilah experience the following:

- Reclusive behavior disguising it as being an introvert
- Missing out on great opportunities because of the fear of being rejected
- Modifying her true identity as an ambitious person to now being shy and timid.
- Self-sabotaging potentially great relationships; pushing people away.
- Shameful because of the incurable STD and regret for losing her virginity to someone who did not reciprocate the equivalent value.
- Depression and possibly suicidal ideologies
- Distrust of men

It is time for Delilah to draw closer to supportive, trusted friends. Transparency and honesty with herself about giving up her virginity to someone who no longer cares for her will be liberating. She is going to have to join a support group for HSV-2 carriers. This will provide her with a clear understanding that her life is not over and there is hope for her future relationships. Delilah will have to forgive and release her sisters from their fiery darts of the past by confronting them once and for all. She is going to have to bring back the happy, ambitious Delilah and Drop her Toxic Past so that she can experience healthy internal and external relationships.

PORNOGRAPHY SCENARIO:

Basheba screamed through the phone at her best friend,

"Porn pisses me off!" Her Bestie asks, "Why? What's wrong? What happened?" Basheba replies, "I caught my husband watching it at 3 am a few months ago; and some other stuff just surfaced last night." "Ugh! It completely destroys healthy sexual communication that we need to have with one another."

Basheba refused to be her husband's deep, dark fantasy. She refused to be Lilly Lollypop and Betty Boom-Boom! Every day, Basheba cried to him, saying, "We can create healthy fantasies together—not you trying to change me into a digital mistress—who has turned you out!" There were days when she would try really hard to get his attention and to please him. She would go so far as to wear bikini swimsuits or sexy lingerie around the house, even while cooking dinner. Sometimes Basheba would hear her husband showering, knock on the door, and ask to join him. He would flat out decline the offer. To make matters worse, her husband suggested that she invest in adult toys in order to fulfill her sexual cravings. Basheba was shocked and totally beside herself. She concluded that all hope was lost concerning their sexual relationship. All of these occurrences left her so confused, unloved, emotionally neglected, and ultimately rejected.

Basheba decided to go to a family and marriage counselor. She invited her husband, for the fifth time, however, he refused to attend. During her counseling session, she gained so much understanding surrounding pornography and its effect on a marriage, as well as the mindset issues of each partner. Basheba reflects on this statement from her counselor, "Porn has a very strong potential to totally disrupt the husband's healthy erection and orgasm level with his mate; leaving both partners unfulfilled and the receiver feeling rejected." Basheba learned that pornography addiction gives the receiving partner a feeling of inadequacies and insecurities. It makes them feel defeated because they can't live up to the performances that the addicted partner loves to watch. She hates that he compared her to his digital mistresses. He said that she was beautiful and attractive but he was not sexually attracted to her. He viewed her as a 'goodie girl' who can't do nasty, grimy things. Basheba blew her top! All she wanted to do was provide fulfillment and enjoyment to her husband but he keeps taking his orgasmic peak to the next level—where no woman can go unless it's him and the screen working together. What a major piece of rejection for Basheba. What should she do? Should she give in to the demands of being a porn star for her husband so that he will become sexually attracted to her? Basheba is caught between a rock and a hard place. She is totally confused and stressed out.

WHY? **Here it is:**

- Lack of 'upfront' communication between the couple concerning each others' needs, desires and expectations surrounding sexual intimacy has created static and confusion.
- Partner's addiction has totally consumed the way he sees sex and how his needs should be fulfilled. There's total disregard for the wife's feelings, wants, sexual and emotional needs.
- More than likely, there was a pornography addiction or casual viewing prior to their marriage and this discussion did not occur during pre-marital counseling.

- The wife feels like she has been betrayed and that she is in this marriage alone. Her self-worth is dwindling.
- The husband did not Drop his Toxic Past, so now it has infected his marriage and overall relationship with his wife.

For help with sexual addictions within a marriage or for Marriage & Family Counseling, go to https://www.psychologyto day.com/ and type in your city for local assistance.

CAUTION: If she gives into being the porn fantasy, she may end up living in a world of regret and resentment. If her heart is not in it, then she will become jealous of the relationship between her husband and any other woman. She will continue to build a wall, consider using toys, or even consent to pornography herself, just to please him. This action will become toxic and possibly lead to divorce. If there is a divorce and Basheba moves on without going through the healing process, then her toxic past of distrust, low self-worth, and wounds of rejection will have a devastating effect on her next relationship.

3

THE DREAM KILLER PAST
FAMILY MEMBERS & FRIENDS

When we were children, going through school and basic life events, our minds began to think about dreams, desires, and our ultimate being or existence in this earth. We were often asked by teachers and other adults, "What do you want to be when you grow up?" With rapid-fire, we spewed out lofty responses such as lawyer, doctor, veterinarian, astronaut, and scientist. We began to look up to and admire people on television, in music entertainment, the movie industry, or social media. As kids, we obsessed over the larger-than-life images portrayed before us and neglected the role models closest to us. Oftentimes, we will have decided on 4-to-5 different career paths even before we get out of middle school. However, there is always this one strong desire in our hearts that will not go away. It either leads us or it pulls us in a specific direction no matter what our mind tells us. Even if someone comes along and attempts to discourage you from your true desire or dream or passion, you know deep down in your heart where you belong.

. . .

BEWARE OF DREAM KILLER VOCABULARY:

Do you really believe that this is going to work?" **Or** "You know that this is a big goal? **Or** It's really hard for people to truly make money doing that. **Or** You know that that's going to cost a lot of money to get it started? **Or** I'm not sure you have what it takes to compete with the 'big dogs' in that industry. **Or** It doesn't take all of that! **Or** Did you think this thing through? **Or** Our family legacy or history does not support that! **Or** We've never done it that way. **Or** I would not do that if I were you. **Or** I think that this is a bad idea.

*SCENARIO: **Terri Linn***

It was a hot summer day filled with excitement, family, and friends. There was cake, balloons, music, and a bunch of 10-year old kids running around the front yard. Terri Linn was so excited and thrilled about the idea of celebrating her 10-year old birthday with all of the traditional birthday frills and games. She was bouncing around on the sidewalk, playing hopscotch and jump rope, trying to pass the time while awaiting the arrival of the rest of her guests. Terri Linn came bouncing down the sidewalk from the porch when she saw a familiar car pull up. It was her aunt and uncle, along with her two younger cousins. She darted towards the car as they were parking and suddenly out jumped her cousins. They gave her hi-fives, Aunt Maggie hugged and kissed her, and then Uncle Harold stepped out of the car. This moment would forever change Terri Linn's life.

'Uncle Harry' is what everyone in the family called him. He was mean, rude, and said whatever came to his mind. Well, Terri Linn got a taste of his rude wrath this day. She bopped around sharing with her aunt and cousins that she was going to be a fashion designer and model. They nodded in agreement because they remember how Terri Linn likes to play dress up, pose for the camera, and help her Mom alter clothing as she sewed on her sewing machine. She showed everyone notebook pictures and sketches of her designs, then began to strut down the sidewalk like a model. Everyone laughed, gave Terri Linn hi-fives, complimented her on the brilliant sketches, and encouraged her to go forward with her dreams—except, you-know-who. Uncle Harry walked up to Terri Linn looked down in her direction and said, "How can you be a model and fashion designer? They only let tall people model. Besides, you have to study in New York and Paris for this type of career. Furthermore, look at your parents' height. Both of them are short and you will not grow any taller than them when you reach the end of puberty. Come up with another dream, kid. You can't do this one, sorry."

Whoa! Her Uncle Harry's words really "took the air out" of Terri Linn's birthday balloons. She was sad and discouraged after Uncle Harry walked away and into the house to greet her parents. Terri Linn was so upset that she tossed her notebook of sketches onto the grass and slid down to the ground in tears. She asked herself, "How can I be so stupid to think that I can be a fashion model and designer? He's right, my parents are short." Her dreams were crushed completely. She had to come up with another plan, dream, ambition, and passion. Terri Linn felt lost.

Six years later, Terri Linn was in her junior year of high school, loving math and accounting. As she searched for colleges, she decided to choose a college with a great business school in order to continue her love of accounting. One year later, Terri Linn graduated with honors, as well as a Business/Math scholarship to attend a great college. Five years later, Terri Lynn graduated with honors and a Bachelor's degree in Business Management and Accounting. She landed a well-paying entry-level Accounting job at a Manhattan, New York firm far from her small hometown of Lima, Ohio.

Terri Linn is now thirty-five, still single, no dependents, a successful senior accountant for the same Manhattan, New York firm, and enjoying her friends as they frequently visited Times Square. She and her friends often get invited to exclusive events, such as Fashion Week and designer debut shows. Terri Linn absolutely loved the buzz, excitement, and viewing the latest fashion coming down the runway. She always says, "I can walk like her, strut like her and wear the hell out of that garment!" So her friend, Eliza, leaned over and whispered to her, "When we get out of here I want to see you do it." Terri Linn took the challenge and strutted down the sidewalk in her stiletto heels. Although her friends laughed, they were truly impressed. Eliza said to her, "Girl, why aren't you a model? You dress so well and wear hot heels every day!" Terri Linn responded, "Are you kidding? I cannot be a model, I am too short. No one wants a petite woman standing at 5'3" and 125 pounds." Eliza reassured her that the times had changed and she could be a model via social media, a print ad model, and break the glass ceiling. Terri Linn dismissed Eliza's encouragement, but these thoughts continued to linger: What if? I wonder what would have happened if I had ignored what Uncle Harry said and pursued a career in fashion? I will never know because it's too late.

WHAT HAPPENED? **Here it is:**

- She believed what her uncle said because he was in authority, he was an adult and he was trusted by the family. His words carried value, even though they were negative.
- She has always been drawn to clothes and fashion, but dismissed it as a simple interest or characteristic of her being.
- She channeled her strengths into a job, which turned into a career. This career is a substitute for her true desires and undiscovered talents.
- She ended up living in the city for which her uncle said she would have to be in order to pursue a fashion career. However, the body height issue continued to push her away from any type of modeling pursuit.
- She did not tell her parents what her Uncle Harry said to her. Therefore, she had no allies or people to counter his negative, dream-killing words.

CAUTION: If she continues to live in regret then it will turn into depression and self-hate. She will hold unforgiveness towards herself as she climbs the corporate latter. She will continue to live a life of false identity and "rerouted strengths" as she pursues her career in Accounting. She will live an unfulfilled life. This may even lead to her living vicariously through her child or someone else who pursued a career in fashion. If she never gets involved in the fashion industry, even to volunteer during Fashion Week, she will continue to live a life of regret and the unknown. Holding on to the unknowns, the what if's and regret can slowly chip away at her confidence. It can also cause her to hold ought and jealously towards people who are succeeding in the industry for which she truly desired to pursue as her own. She must drop her toxic past by forgiving her Uncle Harry for his insensitive, uninformed statements made to her over twenty years ago. Also, she will have to forgive herself for believing these words and allowing them to steer her away from her dreams. She's going to have to find a way to get a taste of the Fashion Industry Life by throwing a fashion week party or volunteering to assist during the event or pursuing a side job of print ad modeling. She must drop her toxic past to experience fulfillment and contentment.

For all of the people reading this, I will let you in on a little secret: there are so many famous and successful People who encountered Dream Killers. Key words: famous and successful. Do your research. You will be surprised! So, keep going and keep pushing forward.

4

THE COLLEGE & CAREER PAST
ROOMMATES. BOYFRIENDS. GIRLFRIENDS. BOSSES.

Attending college can make or break a person. For some people, the experiences may have matured and exposed them to a world of opportunities, networking, and the possibility of leaving a positive legacy to their children. For others, the experiences almost destroyed their mental health and overall well-being, tarnishing their view of college altogether. They wanted to have nothing else to do with college after they finally graduated, and warned everyone else about the pitfalls awaiting them.

Oh, gosh! What a nightmare, huh? Are you still haunted by what you experienced in college or on your first job after college? Many people are living with occasional thoughts about the mistakes they made in college and on their first job. They may be dealing with the overt consequences that continue to resurface, such as DUI's, STD's, babies, fights, Greek Organization pledging-trauma, stalking incidents, failed romantic relationships, bad or inappropriate relationships with professors, fines, credit cards, bad credit, college classmate deaths, drugs and binge drinking. Oftentimes, we reflect on our college days and first jobs when we go to our annual college homecoming to meet former classmates. We take pleasure in swapping war stories with our friends about the "Remember when's..." and "Oh, let me tell you about my first boss and my first job. It was..."

SCENARIO: Roommates

Eve finally made it to her parent's alma mater, as they enthusiastically announced to everyone, "Our daughter is attending the best college in the world!" She was enrolled as a freshman and had declared a major in Chemical Engineering. Eve moved into her dorm, met her three roommates, their parents, and the dormitory house mother. Her roommates were from various parts of the country, such as Kirsten of Albuquerque, New Mexico, Donna of Baltimore, Maryland, and Alice of Huntsville, Alabama. Eve thought to herself, "What a mixture of U.S. Regions in this dorm pod? We are going to have so much fun! I can learn a lot from these ladies." She did exactly that while getting settled in her room-pod.

It took Eve and her roommates three days to move into their pods, decorate and get comfortable in their designated spaces, for which they were well-pleased. Everything was going well for the first month of rooming together. They borrowed little toiletries and hair products from one another, went out to parties and campus gatherings, ate in the Campus Commons at times, and even went to the local mall to hang out and take pictures. They have gotten so comfortable with one another that they began to swap romantic stories about their dates, new love interests, 'getting that money' moments and trying out the new relaxation 'medicine' buzzing around campus. Eve felt so comfortable with her new roomies that she revealed her new 'older-man-adjunct-professor' love interest. Alice smirked, then warned her to be careful with 'messing around' with older men. Eve didn't care, she was totally into him, but she told them they had to keep it a secret. The roomies all giggled and agreed not to tell. They were forming a strong bond with one another.

One afternoon, Eve returned to her room-pod from morning classes. She wanted to take a nap before attending the Campus Community Fireside Chat. Eve got comfortable, texted her lover as a check-in, flopped on the bed, and reached for an eye mask located in her desk drawer. Suddenly, she noticed that things were all out of place in the drawer. She saw envelopes opened, papers shuffled, and a few small items on the floor. Eve was deeply troubled because she knew that she had not left this area in disarray. Eve said to herself, "Who could have gone through my stuff? Oh, no! My money is gone!" She ran out of the room and down the hall to report the theft to the Dorm Mother. By that time, Kirsten and Donna were approaching the hall entrance when they noticed Eve's frustration. She told them what happened but both roomies had strong alibis. Kirsten had spent the night with one of her Ice Cream & Cookies Shop co-workers, where they worked the late shift together. Donna had come in late and left at 7 A.M. for an 8 A.M. Chemistry Lab class, in which Eve was still in the room when she departed. Therefore, the only person remaining was Alice. After about two hours of taking evidence photos, speaking to the police, and making a report, Alice returns to the dorm with a few shopping bags and new jewelry. She was interrogated by the campus police and denied everything. Her story seemed to have a good alibi according to the campus police. The authorities concluded that more than likely it was an outside intruder and one of the roomies forgot to secure the lock on the door. Eve was not convinced that it was an "outside" job. She had her suspicions and her suspicions were going to be proven accurate very soon.

A month goes by, College Homecoming festivities were ramping up and everyone was excited, except Eve. Her lover had started to ghost her and she was still uncomfortable in her dorm pod. It bothered her that she could not trust one of her roommates. She had this feeling that Alice was into more than the suspected theft however, it could not be proven. Nevertheless, all hidden things were going to be revealed very soon.

Eve and Kirsten signed up to join the Homecoming Decorating committee and to be dorm pod door judges. While they were attending the committee meeting, they overheard someone say that Adjunct Professor Fine had been temporarily suspended with pay pending the outcome of an investigation. He was under investigation for having an inappropriate relationship with a female student. Campus police found the two making out in the student's car behind one of the defunct college buildings. Professor Fine was Eve's secret lover, who had been ghosting her. So, Kirsten and Eve walked over and joined the conversation only to get the most devastating news: Professor Fine was caught making out with their roommate, Alice. Wow! Unbelievable! Alice slept with Eve's boyfriend.

They called Donna to tell her the news and pin her location. Donna was in the pod, comforting Alice. Alice was crying to Donna while packing her things and dismantling her area. She revealed to Donna that she was caught cheating on her Sociology exam, therefore she had to move back home. Kirsten whispered over the phone to Donna that Alice was lying and to stall her until they arrived. Once

Eve and Kirsten arrived, they confronted Alice about the exam cheating lies, the money theft, and the fact that she slept with Eve's lover. Alice admitted to all of the accusations and begged them not to report her to the authorities. Eve stormed out of the room and proclaimed that she will never trust and bond with women again, nor fall for dating older men ever.

WHAT HAPPENED? **Here it is:**

- Alice had a sexual relationship with her roommate's boyfriend out of desperation. Alice is very insecure about her non-curvy body type. She feels like her overall appearance and mannerisms are not popular with most guys on campus. It is challenging for her to get the attention of men to whom she is attracted. She has a low self-esteem and low self-worth, which convinced her that using her body is the only way to get someone to like her. She associates sex with love.
- Alice was also jealous of her roommates because they all had love interests and good things happening in their lives.
- Eve was secretly dating an older man, a professor and indulging in an inappropriate relationship because this made her feel adventurous, special and more mature. Finally, she felt in control of her life. On the contrary, she was not in control of anything.
- Eve is like any other young, college student: open to accept and build a friendship. So, she willingly

and whole heartedly trusted all of her roommates. She was not suspicious nor guarded, at first.

- Eve did not expect this level of hurt and betrayal. Therefore, her inner vows to not trust again come from a place of self-preservation. Eve was always the friendly, nice and accepting one in her social circles.

CAUTION: If Eve continues to hold the distrust in her heart for women and refusing to bond with people, she will ultimately miss out on great opportunities for advancement and healing. She will push away potentially great men and women who may have crossed her path for specific reasons. If she holds tight to those inner vows, then they eventually turn into walls. Her walls will keep people, opportunities, healing, and love from getting to her when she truly needs it the most. Also, if she continues to not trust older men, she will push away or miss out on the 'big brothers' and 'mentors' that are not attempting to romanticize the relationship. Eve will have to drop her toxic past, dismiss the inner vows, and give it one more chance to bond with new friends.

SCENARIO: *Boyfriend*

Moses was handsome, 'super fine' according to the ladies, well-dressed, a six-year Pharmacy School major, and not exclusively available to one woman according to the campus rumors. He had plenty of options. Moses or Big Mo is what he preferred to be called by his brotherhood, family members, and close friends, is smart and witty. He uses his smarts for the Pharmacy school academics, but he uses his wit on the "campus streets" to talk his way into an opportunity or talk his way out of a sticky situation. Well, none of this bothered Sarah, for she was intrigued by Big Mo's overall persona. She was attracted to the smart bad boy and elated that he had chosen her as his girlfriend. Sarah felt so special when they walked across campus because almost everyone they passed would call out to Big Mo just to say 'hello.' It was like dating a real-life rockstar!

As the months went by, Big Mo and Sarah's relationship became even more serious and intimate. She moved into his off-campus apartment, drove his car, went grocery shopping for him, cooked, cleaned, and meal prepped for him between her classes. Sarah was so happy and in awe that she could not believe the things that were happening between them. She bragged to her friends about how lucky she was to be with such a wonderful guy with the full package. They planned 'couples' travel during mid-term, winter and Spring break, threw parties, and hosted gatherings as if they were a married couple—until the unthinkable happened.

It was a Friday evening and Big Mo picked up Sarah from the hair salon. He loved to see Sarah experience the luxuries of the spa, nail, and hair salon. So, they were driving along headed to their apartment. Big Mo glanced at Sarah and said, "Wow, you look beautiful! Your hair looks nice. The stylist did a great job!" As Big Mo was complimenting Sarah's hair, he reached over and attempted to rub the back of her hair and neck. Sarah jerks her head towards the passenger side window to avoid Big Mo's fingers in her hair. She said to him, "Hey Babe, I just got a fresh silk press. I don't want to mess up the style." Big Mo slammed on the brakes, quickly took his hands off the steering wheel and they landed on Sarah's face. Big Mo slapped her so hard that she saw stars. As he knocked her into tomorrow, he said to her, "I can touch your damn hair if I want to, I paid for it!" Sarah burst into tears, along with such a loud cry that the neighborhood could hear it. She had now been introduced to the real Big Mo this awful, terrifying day. When they arrived back at the apartment, Big Mo slammed his keys on the kitchen counter, walked to the bedroom, and slammed the door. He left Sarah in the living room, crying and holding her face. Suddenly, Big Mo returned to the kitchen, in a different outfit, grabbed the keys, and left the apartment for hours into the next morning. Sarah was dumbfounded, confused, and wondering how did she land in this nightmare. She thought to herself, "Something else is going on because what I said to him in the car was nothing." Sarah asked herself, "How am I going to get out of this situation?" She was stuck.

A few days passed, but things seemed to get better between them. Big Mo doted on Sarah in front of his brotherhood and friends, he bought her nice clothes and a charm bracelet. Mo assured her that he would not harm her again. He explained that sometimes the pressures of his family legacy to succeed in his academic life weighed heavy on his emotions. Sarah squeezed his hand, rubbed his goatee, kissed his lips and told him that she understood. She promised him that she would always be there for him.

Well, Sarah could not keep that promise, but desperately wanted to. She loved Big Mo, but Big Mo did not love her. After about a month of peaceful intimate days, the occasional slaps started back again and the late nights away 'with the boys' became frequent. Sarah was sad, confused, broken, and alone. Her pain was evident to her friends so much so that her friends had to intervene. They revealed to her that Big Mo was not with 'the boys' every evening, and that actually, he was with another woman. Sarah did not believe her friends until they showed her secret pictures and videos of Big Mo and the other woman. Sarah was absolutely devastated beyond what her mind could handle. She snapped and began to destroy his apartment by breaking mirrors, dishes, cutting up clothes, filling the tub with water until it overflowed, pouring bleach over the rugs, sofa, and carpet. It was truly over for Sarah. She called a friend, grabbed most of her belongings, hopped into the getaway car with her friend, but she eventually spent the next few nights sleeping in a county jail cell.

WHAT HAPPENED? **Here it is:**

- She was already insecure entering into the relationship with Moses. Her self worth and esteem decreased, especially when she compared herself to other women. She could not believe that she could be with "a man like him."
- She based her worth and value on how others treated her when she was a kid, as well as in her young adult life.
- She assumed a specific, exclusive status even though Big Mo never established a status upfront, before she moved in with him. She put all of her trust in him, not expecting for his college campus 'non-exclusive' reputation to affect their relationship.
- Moses' attention and notoriety from others was fuel and energy for her. She believed that she had something special and that she was chosen out of all of his options.

- Sarah compromised her standards, put her life to the side in order to conform to Moses' life. She compromised her values in order to sustain a life with Moses, only to lose what she needed most, her self-esteem.
- Sarah had never experienced the lavish lifestyle in which a college student like Moses lived. She enjoyed having the finer things in life, quality vacations and expensive dinners, as a college student. She became addicted to the reality that was once a childhood dream.

CAUTION: If Sarah tries to remedy her deep hurt, pain, and insecurity by attaching herself to another man, she will ultimately destroy this relationship. She will live with trust issues, defensive behaviors, and fear of domestic violence. There will be a moment where she may accuse this new guy of cheating when he comes home late or does not call during the day. She may even allow herself to be exploited and manipulated so that she can keep this new guy happy and calm. Because Sarah excused Moses' physical and emotional abuse, her standards will allow ill-treatment by others, as well. It is imperative that she refrains from dating for a while, attend domestic violence counseling, consider monthly therapy sessions, and work on clearing her court charges. If Sarah does not heal from this traumatic experience, her toxic past will rule her present life, eventually hindering her from experiencing true love.

SCENARIO: *Girlfriend*

Will was a respectable, Godly, very handsome good guy. He had a great head on his shoulders and a bright future ahead of him. He was not the ladies' man, just looking to date one college girl. Suddenly, Kelly walks into the lecture hall. She was beautiful, sweet, and smart—based on the way she asked questions during the class. Will was completely smitten by her beauty and presence every time they were in their Psychology 101 class together. She had a fragrance that lingered in his nose for days. Her hair was always in the right place, her body was a perfect size and her skin glistened in the sunlight as she walked across campus. It was her smile and eye contact that reeled him into approaching her near the Commons. The rest was history. Will and Kelly were inseparable. If you saw Will, Kelly was somewhere in the vicinity. They spent every waking moment with each other. She comforted him as he completed his frat pledging. She even stood in the hot sun as he practiced with the marching band, waiting to blow him a kiss or give him a wink. Will liked her so much that he invited her to visit his parent's house during an away football game in his hometown. Kelly was excited and felt special.

Their relationship was getting serious, Will expressed his love and shared some very personal stuff about himself with Kelly. Will truly adored Kelly, but she could not reciprocate the love he showed her. Kelly was beautiful, young, and naive. She was being pursued by other college guys, including seniors. She thought this was a big deal. So Kelly broke it off with Will to be with the older, popular college junior. Will was devastated, hurt, and confused.

Two years passed, Kelly got dumped by the older guy and she was filled with hurt. She comes crying back to Will for comfort and in hopes that he would take her back. Will was such a man of integrity that he hugged Kelly, looked her in the eyes, and told her that he could not take her back. He explained to her that he had a girlfriend in which he faithfully liked and could not do her wrong. He told Kelly, "I may marry this girl one day. I do not want to hurt her. As much as I liked you and we shared something special, I've moved on." Kelly was hurt, again.

WHAT HAPPENED? **Here it is:**

- She was so broken and lacking fatherly guidance that she did not recognize a good man who truly loved her and wanted her to experience true love.
- She could not handle his good, positive character due to her poor sense of self.
- Her esteem was deficient. Therefore, any attention from men, whether good or bad, she latched on to it because it gave her a false self-esteem booster.
- He was drawn to her external features and her potential, but did not truly investigate before sharing his secrets. Unbeknownst to him, she underestimated her maturity level, the timing, as well as the responsibility of hearing about his personal life issues.

CAUTION: If Kelly continues to live her life with wounds of rejection, lack of fatherly guidance, and a poor sense of self, then she will continue on a roller coaster ride of emotions. She will travel through life's journey hurting herself, sabotaging potentially great relationships, and hurting others.

Kelly will never experience fulfilling, healthy relationships that her heart truly desires. She must drop her toxic past by seeking counseling or enrolling in therapy sessions that promote consistent healing and growth. Another way to assist in healing, is to bravely face the ugly past. She can research the origin of her father wounds, and ask questions if her parents are still living and/or willing to share the truth. Kelly must forgive herself, daily. One way to accomplish this is by saying aloud, every morning and afternoon, "Kelly, I forgive you and I love you. You are no longer a victim, but a victor in your life's story." (Do this with or without looking into a mirror).

If Will does not release the devastation, hurt, and confusion of Kelly leaving him, he will develop distrust in women. More than likely, he is treading lightly with the woman he is currently dating. Will may become callous and decide to be a 'player' to avoid experiencing any additional hurt or pain. He will make other women pay for what Kelly did to him. He is going to have to drop his toxic past by forgiving Kelly for the hurt she caused him. Will must forgive himself for moving so quickly with Kelly and expecting her to carry the burdens of his personal secrets.

*SCENARIO: **First Job. First Boss.***

Todd was fresh out of college, hired by a prestigious Executive Search firm, living in downtown Chicago with a relatively attractive income. He was ready to roll up his sleeves, grind, make an impression on his boss in order to make a name for himself. During the first month, Todd was always the first to arrive at the firm and almost the last one to leave. He was ambitious but not aggressive. He was a quick learner and extremely smart. He was focused but open to living a little and experience the Chicago nightlife. Todd thought to himself, "I am finally an adult, a real-life adult."

After about six months of grinding, it finally happened, Todd got the attention of his boss, Mr. Melkadeck. He was called into the office and provided an outline of a current project, along with a layout of future plans to add another department. Mr. Melkadeck asked Todd if he was willing to travel in his stead on occasions, conduct a few Standard Operating Procedures (SOPs) presentations on-site and meet with new department staff members for brief training sessions. Todd was blown away! He was speechless about the requests his boss just made to him. He quickly and happily agreed to all of these responsibilities without even asking about overtime pay, work-time expectations, work-life-balance best practices, and other pertinent details. Todd did not care because he had reached his goal of getting the attention of his boss, with the hopes of making a name for himself in the firm.

Todd immediately eliminated his Chicago nightlife outings, his scheduled gatherings with friends, and travel plans to visit his parents. He was "All things Executive Search Firm," where he immersed himself in the fabric of the company daily, nightly, and even on the weekends. Mr. Melkadeck commended Todd on his dedication to the company, ownership of project knowledge, as well as the overall department operations. Mr. Melkadeck went on to tell Todd that he had big things prepared for him if he will continue making great strides in the firm. Todd told Mr. Melkadeck that he was all-in, there for the long haul, and dedicated to the vision of the firm. These were pleasing words to Mr. Melkadeck's ears, so much so that he arranged for Todd to get a bonus check at the end of the month.

Nevertheless, these benefits did not come without some opposition from others in the office. Of course, the seasoned firm associates were not happy with Todd's promotions, bonuses, and accolades. They distanced themselves from him and used sarcastic comments every time Todd would give feedback during team meetings. These petty actions did not bother Todd at all. He had reached his goals with his boss and the firm, therefore he was content. He did not even care if he had one friend. He was happy with being on top. So he thought.

Todd was now four years in the firm with two promotions under his belt. During those years, Mr. Melkadeck surprised him with a new luxury company car and a large bonus check for the holidays. However, he was beginning to question his dedication after a few disagreements and undermining actions of his boss. Nevertheless, he was still Mr. Melkadeck's right-hand-man reaping all of the great benefits of being an executive director in the firm, but something did not feel right. During business trips, Todd witnessed unethical behavior amongst his boss and other top executives. Also, he stumbled upon some paperwork that outlined a soon-to-come buyout of the firm, which did not include any particular severance package for Todd's position. "It is time to go without a doubt," Todd thought to himself. So, he reached out to Abraham, the only friend he had left after bulldozing everyone else out of his life. He told Abraham what he discovered and how he planned to leave his job. Abraham told him to pack up his office items and take a few things home each day. He advised Todd to check on his stock options and any other retirement and savings packages. Then, give two weeks notice and prepare to leave or get forced out before the two weeks arrive.

He took Abraham's advice and scheduled an appointment with Mr. Melkadeck. He submitted his two weeks notice to his boss and thanked him for the opportunity. Mr. Melkadeck was shocked by Todd's resignation and asked him to share the reasons for leaving but Todd's tongue was stuck at the roof of his mouth. Finally, Todd took a deep breath and was truly honest about how he was aware of the buyout plans that did not include his position. He compassionately explained to his boss that he wanted to safely land on his feet. Initially, his boss gave a half-smile, said nothing, and calmly looked at Todd. Then, Mr. Melkadeck picked up the internal office line, called his Office Assistant to step into the office, and asked her to call for security. Todd looked at his boss with quizzical, confusing eyes, leaned to the right side, and said, "Mr. Melkadeck, is everything alright?" His boss said to him that he should not wait for two weeks, but depart today. He told Todd to clean out his office and leave the firm immediately. Mr. Melkadeck concluded the conversation by reminding Todd that he would have never made it without him, he was not smart enough to go any further, he will never get an opportunity like this again, and that he will never get a recommendation from him. Todd's mouth was on the floor. This was a major punch in the gut for him. He could not believe what had happened in that 30-minute meeting which seemed like an eternity. By the time Todd shook off the punch in the gut, the firm security was escorting Todd down the hall to clean out his office. He was so embarrassed because all of this unfolded in front of his division team members.

Everything Abraham warned him of actually happened. He called Abraham when he arrived at his condo. Todd began to vent and say to Abraham, "I gave my blood and sweat to this company! I gave up everything and sacrificed my social life to help this man get to the next level—and look at what he did to me!" Todd continued by saying, "When my boss fired me, it was like he turned into a different person. I cannot believe this! He's not even going to give me a recommendation. I was his right-hand-man!" Todd was upset because he felt a sense of loss and betrayal.

WHAT HAPPENED? **Here it is:**

- Todd's naive and young ambitions led him down a path of hurting himself and hurting others. His dreams and aspirations had no clear outline so he had determined that he would reach them by any means necessary.
- Todd was driven and invested more than what was expected, at first. When these actions were validated by empty accolades, he forfeited all future negotiating power.
- Todd only had himself and his immediate gratification in mind. He forfeited his long term financial security for the thrill of notoriety and leadership.
- Todd lost his support group by cutting off friends and family. These are people who could have provided insight, wisdom and guidance as he climbed the corporate ladder.
- He invested his personal feelings in his boss and the other executives. He did not realize that business is business for them.
- He did not have work-life balance, which clouded his judgement. So, he went full speed ahead and dedicated his life to an entity that did not consider his best interest, at all.

- He wanted control, power and status. More than likely, these were things that Todd admired growing up, desired to have and never achieved them while matriculating through high school and college.

CAUTION: If he does not release the feelings of betrayal and a sense of loss, then he will walk around with a chip on his shoulder. He will most likely experience a grieving process, which can turn into regret, hurt, and depression. He will allow himself to deal with every future situation as a guarded, angry man. These actions will cause him to miss out on opportunities and potentially great working relationships. He will pre-judge people or despise leaders in similar positions to his former boss. His trust level will be at an all-time low. Todd must drop his toxic past before pursuing another high-level job. He must heal by forgiving himself for bulldozing friends and family, forgive his boss for the mean behavior, forge a strong bond with his friend Abraham and reinstate a work-life balance.

5

THE MONEY MISTAKE PAST
YOUR RELATIONSHIP WITH MONEY.

How is your relationship with money? How do you handle money now? How did you handle money when you were younger? Are you someone who lives for money? Or, are you someone who does not care if you have it or not? Do you chase checks and money-making schemes? Did you get sucked into the old College Campus Credit Card trick? Did your parents and church teach you that money is the root of all evil? Did your parents teach you that money should be saved, never taking risks or investing? Did you learn that having just enough for you and your family is all that you need? Do you judge people who are rich or wealthy?

These are real questions that come from real experiences, including my own. One or all of those questions have steered me and many people into destroying others' lives; and in turn the affected people destroy their own lives by entering rehabilitation centers, or premature graves. Nevertheless, there is a bright side: a successful turnaround. Many times our relationship with money originates from how we were introduced to it when we were children. We cannot pick our parents or guardians, nor guard our young hearts against our parents' life lessons about money. Sometimes our parents taught us about money based on the hurt and loss that affected them due to botched money deals or losing their jobs. Just an FYI: Money is NOT the root of all evil. Actually, it's the *love* of money that is the root of all evil; which can be found in the Biblical chapter of I Timothy 6:10. Additionally, our perspective about money was reinforced as we matriculated through high school, got our first part-time job, and then full-time job upon graduation. Nevertheless, this chapter of our lives could be the turning point to uprooting the bad money advice of our parents or guardians. Keep reading. I am going to give you a Bad-to-Worse Money Relationship Scenario and a Bad-to-Good Money Relationship Scenario. Be encouraged.

SCENARIO: *Bad to Worse*

Josh was a single, 35-year old retail store regional manager who had a shoe fetish and a deep craving for travel. Both were the fabric of his being. His apartment closets were filled with designer gym shoes, loafers, custom Italian leather shoes, and the belts to match. His passport had stamps and stickers on top of stamps and stickers—representing five out of the seven continents of the world. You can definitely say that Josh was a world traveler.

Josh was the kind of guy who always landed on his feet when times got rough. He believed that a man only lives once and money is made to be spent. So, he never saved a dime. He did not have investments or a full retirement plan on his job. Moreover, his full annual tax refund checks went towards funding his travel to a new place in the world. He lived life by the seat of his pants. Josh believed that shoes tell the story of a man and traveling to exotic lands is wealth. He believed that investing in his global travel was the best education ever and having the right shoes to do it made the trip even better. Therefore, each time he received his paycheck directly deposited into his account, it was spending time. Josh paid his bills, bought groceries, ordered a pair of shoes, spent a few dollars at the local adult entertainment club, bought travel literature, and put a few dollars in his 'travel savings account' for his upcoming trip. His annual travel schedule was to take off in March or April for a short Spring trip, explore another part of the world in June or July for a Summer trip and close out the year in November or December with his Winter Trip. Life was good for Josh, so he thought.

It was time to pack for his Summer trip to Greece. Somehow, back in April, Josh stumbled upon a travel group for solo travelers where they needed a replacement for an open slot. Josh agreed upon this non-refundable, deal of a lifetime. He was so thrilled that he saved over a grand by agreeing to be a substitute traveler to Greece! No way was he going to pass up this deal. He truly did not care that it was non-refundable; besides, what would happen in three months that would cause him to cancel? This...

Josh decided to hang out with a few of his gym buddies to hike and mountain climb. This always provided relaxation and a clearing of the mind for Josh before he made his global trek. The four gym rats set out on their usual hiking trail, laughing, joking, and swapping weight lifting stories along the way. They were only thirty minutes into the trip when lightning, thunder, and heavy rain came out of nowhere. The guys tried to run for shelter, dodging brush, branches and leaping over sticks and logs. When all of a sudden, the unthinkable happened—Josh leaped over a log, stepped on a sharp rock, and slipped on wet tree leaves. He fell backward due to the weight of his backpack. He landed on the backpack and the log, cracked his skull, and dislocated a spinal disc. His friends rendered aid and called the park ranger. Josh was airlifted to the closest trauma center where he remained for two months. When he was released from the hospital, Josh was sent to a rehabilitation center to learn how to walk again.

When Josh gathered his senses and regained full consciousness, he realized that he was on the verge of losing everything. Of course, he lost his trip to Greece and unfortunately, the temporary use of his lower back. He had to resign from his job, apply for unemployment and disability support. Josh had to swallow his pride and seek financial assistance from his family to pay past due bills and save his apartment for a few months until he relocated to an assisted living facility. As he sat in the rehabilitation center, he thought to himself, "How in the hell did I get here? How is it that now I'm a charity case?" Josh felt so much embarrassment, as well as regret in his heart. He wanted to kick himself for his former beliefs and practices with money. He sat in his wheelchair, gripping his back brace, looking out at the blue sky wishing that he could turn back the clock. He begged God to end this nightmare.

WHAT HAPPENED? **Here it is:**

- Josh lived a life without balance. It's great to have a "live-life-to-the-fullest" belief system. However, in the process of living life, one must use wisdom and save money. One must prepare for the 'raining days' with an Emergency Fund and ensure that your "living life to the fullest" practices do not become a burden for family and friends.

- Josh was taught that money was made to be spent but missed the other parts of his money lesson: Earn, Save, Spend, Give and Invest.
- He was very familiar with good things happening to him. He became comfortable with the illusion that he would always land on his feet. Therefore, preparation for the longterm future was not an immediate goal.
- He did not have dependents, nor did he have assets in his name. Therefore, this gave him a false sense of security that he was free to recklessly spend money on only himself.
- Josh was selfish, felt invincible and lacked wisdom.

CAUTION: If he continues to live with regret and embarrassment in his heart, then these two toxic emotions will slowly destroy his confidence and health. It will slow down his physical healing process causing his mobility to be stunted. Regret may also propel him to live in the past and possibly blame his parents for not doing a better job of teaching him how to manage his money. Embarrassment may cause him to retreat and pull away from his gym buddies. He is embarrassed because he can no longer flex his body in the gym. Instead of feeding off their physical mobility energy and galvanizing their fitness motivation, he wallows in self-pity. Regret and embarrassment will cause Josh to make more selfish decisions which may lead to a deeper hole of depression. If Josh does not drop his toxic past and forgive himself for making money management mistakes, then he will go through life missing out on many beneficial opportunities to heal and to grow.

*Scenario: **Bad-to-Good. In my own words...***

As I look back over some twenty years of my adult life, I shake my head in total dismay and disappointment at how many opportunities I missed because of wrong teachings, naive business dealings, erroneous guidance, and fear of lack or insufficiency. I could kick myself for all of the money that I lost, threw away, and mismanaged because I did not align myself with the leadings of God, the right people, and knowledge. I remember owning lucrative real estate. At one given time, I owned and operated as a landlord, three beautiful residential properties. I allowed my personal emotions to get in the way of the mindset that "business is business." with my business partners and tenants. I convinced myself that I was not designed to be a shrewd business person. Therefore, when the 2008 housing market crashed, I crashed along with it. I totally gave up on real estate investing, made an inner vow that I would never go back into owning property again, and fought tooth-and-nail to offload what I owned. During the offloading, I made a nice profit from the first property, broke-even on the second property and I had to conduct a short-sale contract on the third one. Wow! Was I upset or what? Yes, my credit had a huge Short-Sale ding on it and decreased my credit score to the 600's. I thought that I was ruined. So much regret filled my heart, which made my stomach feel like there was a deep hole in it. I shook my head in disbelief and asked myself, "How do I recover?" With no other relief in sight, I told myself to just "wait it out" and be patient. That is exactly what I did.

Over the next ten years, I changed my thinking about money. I secured a full-time job, got a promotion, cleaned up my credit, paid off bills and credit cards, saved my money, established two IRA's, invested in stocks, created an LLC, and built up my non-profit organization. In my eyes, this was security and comfort. I felt safe and in control for the time being. About one year later, my spirit was unsettled and my heart was yearning to be a homeowner again. I knew that this was the wise and smart thing to do. I knew that I was wasting money renting this elaborate townhouse in downtown Atlanta. Additionally, I wanted to own residential and commercial real estate. So, I set out to begin the process. This time, I prayed and allowed God to guide me to the right people and beneficial programs that would align with God's will for my life. I began to educate myself by joining a business coaching program, investing in one-on-one business coaching, completing a 21-day financial health course, attending home buying webinars, researching equitable properties around the city, reading credible business articles, and following successful investment/real estate business entrepreneurs on various social media platforms.

As I learned from the real estate experts, I continued to pray and seek God for the right timing and approach in this area. It was always in my heart to help the community with my nonprofit, but also with my For-Profit business. Being a giver and living with purpose is innate for me; it's how God created me. Therefore, one morning, I remember hearing in my spirit specific details about how to structure my LLC, especially the real estate division of it. After writing out the structure, I got excited and highly motivated to get started. The details were clear, the business plan was simple and the resources were established. I knew that this was my turning point in finally experiencing long-lasting victory. Nevertheless, before diving headfirst, I signed up for a Business Mentor with the Small Business Administration. It was one of the best decisions that I made, aside from joining the business coaching class. As I shared my dreams, visions, goals, and plans, my mentor took it and "ran with it." My business mentor walked me through this journey step-by-step until I reached the end zone and made a touchdown. Now, I own and operate an enterprise with three For Profit businesses and one nonprofit 501c3 organization.

WHAT HAPPENED? **Here it is:**

- I was taught to hold on to my money and save as much as I could save. I was told, "You are all that you have. Do not depend on others to save you."
- At one particular time in my young adulthood, I made a foolish decision, took a foolish risk and ended up homeless for two weeks. For that period of time, I slept in my car or on the floor of my friends' apartments when their boyfriends were not there. My mother, sister and college friend, Michelle, had to bail me out. This short occurrence of financial lack caused me to make inner vows that I will never be homeless again and no one will ever have to bail me out. Although I lived up to this vow, it caused me to remain stuck for twenty years. It caused me to hold on to my money, hardly investing in anything.

- I have a big heart and mixed it with 'no balance.' Therefore, I gave out to so many people, trying to save the world and losing in the end.
- When I became an independent contractor back in the late 90's, I began to make more money than I ever dreamed. The benefits were outstanding! However, I had no guidance. I mismanaged my money by not setting a budget early on when I started to make lots of non-taxed money. I paid the taxes on it, spent the rest—instead of investing some of it.
- I left God out of my decisions.

CAUTION: If I had not dropped my toxic past and pride, then I would not have asked God for help, nor my coach and mentors. My past mistakes and teachings would have continued to lead me down a path of false security and believing in my abilities. I would continue to carry regret and disappointment, which would block me from what God had planned for me. He has an expected end for me—one that is filled with good and no sorrow or financial lack. I realized that there is no lack in the Kingdom of God and Heaven is not bankrupt. Had I not dropped my toxic past, then I would not have entered a journey of God's goodness that is filled with great business and personal relationships, as well as sustainable success.

6

THE EX PAST
FRIEND. FIANCÉ. FIANCEE. SPOUSE.

Are you holding on to what your ex-spouse did to you? Are you holding on to what you did to your ex-spouse? Are you reliving the hurt and pain experienced during the breakup? Are you asking yourself how on earth did you get connected to this person in the first place? Is it hard for you to forget about the good and bad times you spent with this person? Are you overwhelmed by regret, guilt, and shame caused by a damaged relationship or public divorce? Are you regretting that you went through with the divorce? Do you regret some of the decisions you made while in the relationship? Do you regret how you handled the breakup? Are you feeling a sense of guilt and shame because of other people's comments and questions about your failed relationship?

Breakups can be extremely painful and life-altering. Whether your partner broke it off with you or you willingly separated from your partner, both actions produce hurt, pain, and sometimes confusion. The pain can seem unbearable and unbelievable when it first happens. It can seem unbelievable, especially if you truly cared for this person and they seemingly pulled away at an instant—leaving you confused with unanswered questions. Then, you begin to convince yourself that maybe it was your fault or that something is wrong with you. Many negative thoughts begin to ensue, such as: "I cannot make it without this person." Or, "I cannot see myself ever living a life without them in it."

Sometimes separation can cause one to feel as if all hope is lost—especially divorce. Divorce is like experiencing death. Oftentimes there is a period of grieving, depression, and despair. Your emotions are on a rollercoaster ride to nowhere positive, only down in the dumps. Separating from someone with whom you were fully one and intimate is devastating. But let me warn you.

Don't stay in the dumps. Don't stay down and out. It's dangerous and harmful to your health, as well as your future. It's time to free your spirit from these debilitating emotions. It is time to free your mind of these traumatic, haunting memories. It is time to release the regret, guilt, and shame that can potentially stunt your growth. Let's see if these scenarios can help you move forward.

SCENARIO: *Ex-friend (non-married partner)*

They had been best friends for at least three years before things turned romantic between them. Chuck had been there for Lydia during all of her breakups and relationship "growing pains." Lydia had been truly supportive to Chuck during his failed engagement, business ventures, job promotions, and minor health challenges. They provided each other with spiritual advice, financial guidance, personal relationship advice, as well as overall emotional support. Chuck and Lydia were such good friends to one another, especially during family deaths and tragedies. Any negative thing that occurred in either one of their lives, they came to each others' aid. They would set each other up on dates with colleagues, friends, or church buddies. If things did not go well on that first or second date, they would console each other and laugh about the events of the date. Chuck and Lydia were such good, mature friends that when either one had to use their friend's restroom for an extended time, the odor or timeframe was never an embarrassment. They were so comfortable with one another's presence, existence, and space. Maybe too comfortable.

One evening, Chuck hosted a fifteen-person, small gathering at his home. It was a book release party for his good friends, Bethany and Rod. They had co-authored a book about servanthood and metaphorically washing each others' feet as an act of compassion. As they were wrapping up the book event, Rod decided to demonstrate the title by washing Bethany's feet. He demonstrated how Jesus washed the feet of his disciples and how Mary Magdalene wiped the feet of Jesus with oil. The audience was moved with different emotions, some with tears. Then, Rod dared Chuck to follow his example and to choose someone's feet to wash. Chuck accepted the challenge and whispered to his buddy that he would choose Lydia because she was mature and would not misunderstand the foot-washing as would some other women in the room. Chuck places the bucket near Lydia's feet, removes her shoes, and slowly lifts one foot above the bucket of water to begin the foot-washing. He looks up at her, prays a prayer, she gazes into his eyes and smiles. At that moment, Lydia's emotions went crazy for Chuck. She knew that he was compassionate and an all-around good guy, but this moment took her to another stratosphere with him. Lydia melted, bit her bottom-lip, and allowed one tear to roll down her face. When he finished,

Lydia tried to pretend that her tear was for the book demonstration, only. So, she jumped up and proclaimed to the audience, in a jovial voice, "Wow, that was a powerful demonstration!" Everyone agreed, clapped, and began to depart for the evening.

Lydia decided to leave along with the other guests, to escape the weird feeling that she suddenly developed for Chuck. Normally, she would have remained after the event to help clean up, but not this time. As Lydia arrived home, Chuck called and they chatted about the success of the Book Release Party. They laughed, talked about the next steps with Bethany and Rod's book, as well as how they would support them. Suddenly, Lydia heard the doorbell ring, she asked Chuck to hold on as she answered the door. She peeped out and laughed into the phone. It was Chuck. He stepped into her foyer, asked her why she left so soon, and told her that the foot-washing made him feel a little closer to her. Lydia agreed and they began to kiss. They made their way to her bedroom and slowly removed each other's clothes. Chuck was very gentle with Lydia because he knew that she had been abstinent for five years. He kissed her feet, legs, inner thighs, and made his way up to her breasts. As Chuck reached for the golden square packet of protection, he looked into Lydia's eyes and asked if she was ready. Lydia replied, "Yes, I am ready. I trust you with my life." As Chuck gently thrust himself inside of Lydia, she wept and moaned the words, "I love you." Lydia's thoughts ran wild for him. She knew that their strong friendship planted Chuck halfway in her heart, now this intimate moment made her believe that it was 100% sealed. "I am all yours," she whispered to him as they made passionate love.

The next day, as they awakened, feelings of regret washed over both of them. Chuck asked Lydia why did she allow him to break her five-year abstinence period. She told him that it felt right because they were such great friends and that they had shared so many genuine, intimate moments like no other relationship. After a bit of discussion, they both agreed that it felt right, they should be together, but they had crossed the friendship line. Things had become complicated and in need of sorting out. They had gone against their principles and standards about waiting and dating. They agreed to remove sex from the equation, date each other the right way, and wait until they were married. Did it work?

The dating plan lasted six months until Chuck had a sudden relapse in his health. He was hospitalized for an extended time. Chuck and his parents removed all visitation and calls, including Lydia. She begged to see him, but all parties refused; citing that he needed to be clear of external germs. She was devastated. Confusion and worry overwhelmed her to the point of depression. These emotions drove her to make the most drastic decision ever: to move away and take a job in another region of the country. She sought spiritual counsel, as well as therapy to see if this would change her mind about moving, however, both the therapist and church counselor encouraged her to move forward, cleanse her heart and try to gain closure. Lydia thought it over and convinced herself that maybe this relocation is the best idea and new scenery would help her get over the rejection and pain; but, it did not. Lydia continued to reach out by phone, leaving voice mail messages and sending letters to Chuck's house. No answer, no response. She was crushed.

One year later, Lydia was comfortably settled in her new job, home, and community. She met new friends and spiritual groups at the local church. Although Lydia had moved forward physically and mentally, she had not dated anyone out of fear of rejection and the desire to heal. One day, while shopping for her office holiday party, memories of Chuck flashed across her mind. She decided to give it one last try to talk to him—just to gain closure. So she reached out to Chuck to find out if she could get through to speak to him and check on his well-being. Suddenly, someone answered the phone. It was Chuck! She finally got through—only to find out that he had been released from the hospital about two months after she left town.

During the call, he revealed the reason behind blocking her calls and visitation. He explained that he was afraid his life was over and did not want her to experience this type of pain. He shared with Lydia that his health-relapse was so severe the doctors were not hopeful, and that he and his parents were scared of the prognosis, as well as the surgery. He deliberately pushed her away because he felt that she was too good of a woman for this type of burden. He felt like she had her entire life ahead of her. This life should be for someone else, who was deserving of her goodness. Lydia cried to Chuck, telling him that she would liquidate everything and move back to be with him. That's when he revealed to her that he was engaged and going to be married in three weeks. Lydia begged him not to do it but to no avail. He told Lydia that he loved this woman and that she was his soulmate. He told Lydia that this woman was the one for him. They had known each other since high school, however, they hadn't made a connection until she was assigned to be his nurse in the hospital. Lydia sobbed into the phone, overwhelmed by feelings of loss and conviction. The pain and regret of crossing friendship boundaries knocked her to the floor in the store. She wished that she had not allowed herself to cross the friendship line. She thought herself, "Gosh, I can't believe he is gone. Damn, this hurts!" Closure with Chuck came wrapped in a black bow for Lydia. This felt like death to her. It was officially over.

WHAT HAPPENED? **Here it is:**

- Chuck placed Lydia in the friend zone of his life, but relied on her as his friend, everyday traveling companion and confidante. He trusted her on the level of one of his best male friends.
- Lydia placed Chuck in the friend zone of her life, but relied on him as her confidante, relationship coach, and emotional dumping ground.
- They were comfortable with each other, ignoring the obvious signs of chemistry between them. They did not address their close friendship until it was too late.
- Both parties did not initially communicate about their friendship, its value and worth to one another. They both assumed something totally different about their friendship.
- Lydia felt closer to Chuck than he did to her; for he would have trusted her with his health challenges and hospital visitations.
- Chuck cares about Lydia's well-being, therefore, he pushed her away even when she was willing to come back into his life. He is comfortable with the nurse because she has a compassion for medicine (his immediate need), as well as witnessed him in his most vulnerable state.
- The sexual encounter totally destroyed the purity of their authentic friendship.

- Sex solidified the friendship and moved it forward for Lydia; Sex satisfied and defined the friendship for Chuck. For him, it completed the pursuit of fully knowing Lydia.

CAUTION: Obviously, Chuck has moved on with his life. However, Lydia is picking at her wounds, licking her wounds, and living in yesterday for Chuck. If she doesn't drop her toxic past, then she will totally miss out on the best years of her life. As a form of self-preservation and protection, Lydia may make inner vows and put up walls to keep people away from her. Or, she will allow her infected, emotional wounds to infect the lives of others around her— which will prevent her from having healthy relationships with both men and women. A vicious cycle of failed relationships will continue for years to come.

Lydia will carry in her heart **unforgiveness** for Chuck's actions, regret for giving up her five-year abstinence to him, and the betrayal of their intimate, close friendship for someone else. She may even begin to develop an angry disposition with God. She may feel as if God let her down by not protecting her heart. Lydia may need to seek therapy and spiritual counseling to help her heal from this traumatic breakup. She will need to learn how to forgive herself and others. Lydia will want to gain an understanding of the fact that mistakes were made and that she can recover from those mistakes. Lydia will need to learn that she can start over, start anew, and open her heart to experience true love.

Scenario: *Ex-spouse*

He found the love of his life, so he thought. Jobe was ready to settle down with Nala. One part of him was convinced that he needed a life partner to settle his heart, another part of him wanted to ensure that Nala would always be there, and the third part of him gave in to the pressures of his family and friends that it was time to get married. They always said to him, "You are not getting any younger." "Face the truth, you are in your late thirties and it's time to have kids."

Nala and Jobe were intellectually and professionally compatible. He was attracted to Nala's intelligence, attentiveness, beauty, and many other surface things they had in common. Jobe enjoyed Nala's company and conversation. He thought that she was as beautiful as an Egyptian queen. Nala reciprocated the sentiments towards Jobe. She was attracted to his giving heart to others. She thought that he was truly handsome, super smart, funny, well-dressed, as well as outright sexy. So, they tied the knot.

A few months into their marriage, Jobe decided to confront Nala about the lack of sex and affection between them. Every time Jobe tried to initiate affectionate, intimate moments with Nala, she would fake sleep, claim a headache, remain in the home office, suggest a movie, or avoid him altogether. Jobe could count on one hand the number of times they had had sex since their wedding night and honeymoon. You see, during their courting and engagement, they agreed on waiting to be intimate until their wedding day. Jobe and Nala were excited about this decision, so why has there been a change in Nala? Jobe went downstairs to the home office to confront her.

Nala was pecking away on the laptop, deeply engrossed in this important event that she was co-hosting with her best friend. Jobe stepped into the office, sat down directly in front of Nala, and told her that he needed to get some things off his chest. In slow motion, Nala stopped typing, looked up at Jobe with large eyes, and said, "Ok, honey. What's up?" Jobe told Nala that the lack of sex between them is not going to work. He asked her if she had issues with their past sexual moments or with his performance. Nala said to Jobe, "Honey, I love you so much. I think that you are handsome and sexy." "Babe, there are just some things going on with me getting in the mood, getting aroused...you know? It's not you." Jobe told Nala that he could help her get in the mood with some new techniques. He told her that it is not right for a vibrant, young couple not to have sex. She agreed but came up with no solutions. Jobe walked out of the office, furious with Nala. He knew there was something else—he just could not put his finger on it at that moment.

Another month passed, no sex or affection from Nala— just kisses and hugs as they would come and go, throughout the day. Now and then, she would swat him on the butt or grab his pecks while he got dressed for work. Jobe could not take it anymore, so he set out to find solutions. He called one of his close friends and confidante. He told him about their sexless marriage, the talk they had in the home office and the days she would fall asleep on the sofa with the computer on her lap. Jobe's friend hesitantly said to him, "Man, she might be with someone else." Jobe quickly denied this notion to avoid the haunting thoughts soon to follow. A little part of him believed the thought that Nala might be cheating on him. So, he left work, dug around the house, and suddenly located a few items securely tucked away in the back of his wife's closet. He found her battery-operated secret lover packed in a cute black satin drawstring bag—unbelievable! It all made sense, now. Jobe suddenly remembered how Nala would never allow him to join her in the shower or that she would get up in the middle of the night to pretend to work in the home office. Jobe chuckled for a moment at this discovery but quickly turned angry. He said to himself, "I wonder what's turning her on besides her thoughts?" Jobe called his buddy for some advice. His buddy told him that sometimes women watch porn just like us, as well as hide things in places they know we will not go—the feminine hygiene cabinet.

So, Jobe went to look in her lady parts drawers and cabinet for hidden stuff. There it was—a USB flash drive. He rushed to the computer to see what was on this flash drive. He hit the roof when he saw the contents stored on this tiny piece of equipment. There were scanned birthday cards, copied emails, saved text messages, as well as old vacation pics of her and another guy! After combing through dozens of documents and photos, Jobe discovered that Nala had not only been watching porn, but she had not broken up with her former fling. Evidently, Nala and this guy met while she was dating Jobe. She continued to see him, never broke it off with him, planned secret trips with him, and engaged in self-pleasure while they were apart. Jobe was boiling with anger.

Jobe called his buddy to tell him of the discovery. His buddy told him not to confront her about what he found, take it easy, and play it cool. He told him to put back all of the evidence perfectly and unsuspecting. His buddy told him to call her, set up a dinner date, but to meet at the restaurant directly after work. So, Jobe went back to work to follow through with the suggested plans. That evening, they met at the local restaurant, had dinner, discussed vacation plans, and followed each other home. Throughout the night, Jobe never mentioned anything, nor did he give a clue what he had discovered about Nala. He just flirted with her to see if she would reciprocate. Nala gave Nothing!

They went about their same routine for preparing to go to bed, but this time Jobe asked Nala to take a shower with him. She quickly said, "How about I draw you a bath, wash your back, massage your feet and rub your head?" Jobe declined, took his shower, and went to bed. Nala showered, walked downstairs to the home office, fired up the laptop, then fell asleep on the sofa.

One year had passed without much success in their marriage. Jobe had not found a way to confront Nala without appearing to be a crazy husband, snooping around in her underwear drawer. So, they tried counseling and sexual health therapy, to no avail. Jobe was not only discouraged with his wife's emotional neglect but sexually frustrated. He loved Nala with all of his heart. He was taught to love his wife unconditionally and to exhaust all resources to save the marriage. He was done! He began to talk to his buddy about possible divorce options, as well as the ramifications. He thought to himself, "Thank God we don't have any kids because this would be messy."

No sooner than he finished discussing divorce options with his friend, Nala calls him at work to set up a family meeting. That evening during the meeting, Nala comes clean with Jobe about the affair with the other guy. Nala's other guy no longer wanted to share her with Jobe. She tells him that they should get a divorce because she is no good for him. She tells him that she cannot be the woman that he needs and envisioned for his life's happiness. She apologizes for being a neglectful and disrespectful wife, wasting his time for too long. She cried to him, "You do not deserve this kind of treatment. You were so patient with me." On one hand, Jobe was relieved because this was like an answered prayer, and on the other hand, he was deeply disappointed by this upcoming separation. They agreed to get a divorce.

WHAT HAPPENED? **Here it is:**

- There was not a true love and friendship between Jobe and Nala. Jobe did not have a solid grasp on what it meant to "find true love." He found someone who gave him a bit of peace in his heart and chemistry, along with the surface qualifications.
- Marriage was a business decision for Nala. She never really loved Jobe. She desired security, protection, as well as assistance with everyday living expenses. It was a strong possibility that Nala had some financial goals or spending habits that were made a reality due to marriage support (Jobe is her meal ticket).
- They missed marriage counseling altogether. This would have exposed their true desires and life goals. It would have delayed the marriage or caused them to fully develop a friendship.
- Nala met the man of her dreams while dating Jobe, but was not honest enough to break it off with either man, nor effectively communicate her feelings. She saw opportunity and weakness in both men. She took advantage of them for her selfish gain.
- Jobe missed the red flags while they were dating. Nala never expressed a deep love and connection with Jobe. She was attracted to his giving heart, which could have been anyone along the way.

- There was not a spiritual connection, nor a moral foundation between them.
- They allowed external pressures to convince them that it was the right time to get married, instead of waiting and having lengthy conversations. Bottom line: they were not ready to settle down into a marriage.

CAUTION: If Jobe does not drop his toxic past and the mistakes he made in this short marriage, his healing process will take longer than it should. Jobe will place all women in a category avoiding or resisting the opportunity to interact with them. He will put up walls, make inner vows, and possibly become callous or dismissive towards these women. Jobe will miss out on opportunities to build friendships along the way. He may play the nonchalant role, pretending as if he does not want to get married or be in a committed relationship anymore.

Somewhere along the way, after time has passed, Jobe will live in regret—which is dangerously toxic to the health. It will plague his thoughts with this notion: Something is wrong with me. Unforgiveness will overwhelm Jobe in the form of beating himself up for missing tale-tell signs while dating Nala. On the other hand, Jobe may close this part off and pretend to be ok. Then, begin to 'rebound-date' women to get over Nala. Jobe may even decide to get married shortly after his divorce, carrying all of his buried hurts and pain into this new marriage. In turn, the vicious, toxic cycle continues.

7

THE AFFAIR PAST
COUNTERFEIT LOVE

Her money was stacked, her fitness and body goals accomplished, the business was booming, and she was ready for summer vacation. Kandace had planned two months of summer fun, but never expected that it would include hot summer love. Oooh, my goodness, this definitely caught Kandace by surprise. *Unexpected* is the only word to describe what would happen next during her hot summer days. It was the first of July and the temperature was rising between two rulers of the jungle.

Those hot summer days turned into eight months of passionate nights and twilight rendezvous' with him—the unhappily married man. It was bliss. The chemistry and connection between them were off the charts. It was something out of a Hollywood movie. The connection was so strong that they finished each others' sentences, thoughts and physical advances. During the day, they would even text each other at the same time to check-in. Her mind was blown. Kandace was smitten.

Their passion and heated love continued into the Fall season and Kandace was intoxicated, hooked, addicted, or whatever you want to call it—she was his and there was no turning back. Nothing else mattered to her because the unhappily married man was happy in her presence. She was his place of peace. They talked three to four times per day, texted every chance they could get in the day and talked **until 2 o'clock or even sometimes 3 o'clock** (the wee hours of the morning) in the morning. Every physical moment he could carve out of his day, he slipped away to see Kandace, if only for a kiss, a back rub, or a deep, long hug. She was all his—*so she thought*. Hindsight, he was "love bombing" her by showering her with attention and affection at the highest level.

The winter season brings family gatherings, holidays and celebratory parties. Well, the seasonal events approached and things began to cool off a bit. Kandace realized that she was now the last person in his equation of life when his routine family responsibilities were in question. A cold reality began to set in for Kandace. She was frozen in time, wishing that those hot, steamy summer nights would return to thaw her out. Unfortunately, the flame had been extinguished between them—at his subtle request and behavior.

Spring is here. He was distant, physically gone, very little contact and no regard for Kandace, nowadays . Pools of spiritual and emotional blood poured from her body. She was wounded from her head to her vagina because of his sudden silence and short text responses. She felt numb. The pit of her stomach was aching from regret of being vulnerable with him.

During their affair, he had claimed her body as his own because she gave it to him in word and in actions. She had pledged her true love to him in text and verbally, therefore, whatever he wanted, she gave it to him. She had submitted every ounce of her being to him and he knew it. She was his toy and silly putty in his hands. However, that was not enough to keep him coming around. He was gone and he took her heart with him. Kandace tried to double back to retrieve her heart, just one piece of him, and a few beautiful memories by reaching out every now and then; but, it was no use. It was completely over—he removed her from his social media view and ignored her once-per-month text messages. Damn, he was gone. Kandace couldn't believe it. He was truly gone. The king of the jungle carried a third of her heart back to his den burying it under bush debris. He was gone!

The affair, the connection, the chemistry, and the contact with him was like no other occurrence Kandace had ever experienced. His absence bothered her to depths and abysmal levels that were so new to her that she did not know how to cope. So, Kandace had to survive this spiritual divorce by doing the only thing she knew to do...write. She opened a fresh, brand new journal and began to pour out her thoughts, feelings, emotions, prayers and the Godly lessons she believed The Most High was dropping in her spirit.

Kandace's Self-reflection Journal and Godly Lessons— written as they occurred:

As you read Kandace's thoughts, please try not to judge her. You will walk with her through mental withdrawals and emotional rollercoasters.

HEALING JOURNEY | **Day One**

I feel like weeping, vomiting and hiding in my closet forever. I did it—something that was wrong and selfish. I betrayed myself, my values, my morals and what God tried to instill within me earlier this year—Proverbs 5:15 English Standard Version "Drink water from your own cistern, flowing water from your own well."

THE STING IS REAL. The rejection is irritating. I expected this, but I wasn't ready to feel the poke of the needle—never!

It's my fault. I want so much for it to be his fault, but I knew what I was walking into. I selfishly walked into this 8-month affair hungry and thirsty from being starved of male affection, love, attention, and sex—while wandering in the wilderness.

HEALING JOURNEY | **Day Two**

I expected that this wouldn't last. That he would reject me; I mentally told myself all of this—but I reneged on the promise to my emotions and mental psyche. I reneged on the inner vow I made to myself. I want so much for this to be a perfect separation, but it stings. I want so much to be angry with him but it's not his fault. He was being a hunter in the wilderness. He stalked his prey, ate what he wanted and left me licking my wounds. Why? How? Because I wasn't fully armored up. I let him in with arms open wide and breastplate down—not protecting my heart. I am angry with myself because I know better. I KNOW BETTER! I know that I should have been girded up and strong. But my weariness and anger at God took precedence.

Now, I want him to totally not affect my existence anymore. I want every memory of this man to fizzle with the wind. I want him to disappear. I want him to be figment of my brief imagination. Ugh...I weep for my myself, my igno-rance, my emotions, my stupidity, and my selfish act. I traded my wilderness experience with God for selfish, temporary passion. I traded my wilderness experience, my soon to escape and exodus experience for eight months of forbidden, unthinkable pleasure.

The sting is throbbing and the wound is swollen.

Now, it's time for me to pick my ass up off this wilderness floor, heal from self-inflicted wounds and get out of this wilderness maze once and for all. I even asked God to make me immune to his recent distance and lack of communication. I don't want it to phase me. I don't want to care about it. No more renting free space in my mind. I am no longer for sale.

HEALING JOURNEY | Day Three

His rejection was subtle; his message of "lack of interest" was slow and calculating. He would not take my "out" that I was trying to give him. He would not admit that he had moved on from me. He was weak and would rather try and kill this connection slowly, silently, passively, and softly. But it's painfully obvious, simply bullshit and disrespectful. (*My inner being speaks, "Really, girl? What respect? Pleeeeease, you disrespected yourself when you slept with this married man."*). So I erased his digital footprints from my phone and computer.

It's time to rid myself from the residue of this man. I want his scent erased off my life, completely.

HEALING JOURNEY | Day Four

I am checking his IG, Facebook and my phone for text messages. Yup, I fell back into this bowl of bullshit that I cooked up for myself. He is my kryptonite. So, I reinstated some of his digital residue to get just a glimpse of his mysterious, beautiful eyes and a whiff of his essence. Now, I have to keep telling myself, "Leave him alone. Stop reaching out to him!" He needs God to speak to him and to deal with his twisted views on relationships and deception of being unfaithful. I have to place my heart in God's hands and allow God to flood me with His Goodness and favor. I have to continuously tell myself, "Get this through your thick head, "He is done with you!"

He only wanted me for sex and to extinguish his intrigue. He will not risk his marriage on me. I am not valuable to him. I must go on and be at peace. This is not my life. This is not who I am. I am better than this. How did I let this happen? Why can't I stop thinking about him?

Lesson and takeaway: I allowed him to pierce my armor and my heart. My armor was weak and too big. Now, that I am slowly healing from this huge mistake, I have to get fitted for the upcoming battles, the fights and the war. Because, he may circle back for a late night rendezvous. He is my kryptonite that makes me weak.

HEALING JOURNEY | **Day Five**

As I was at work and typing an email, this thought came to me to help me further understand and heal: He was keeping me warm until his next adventure and bucket list check-off. However, my absence from his life will bring scars and wounds to his psyche and soul. He met a unique spirit within me and his life was at a sense of peace that he couldn't pinpoint the origin until now. I gave him delight, escape and insight. He's reliving the messages and where he went wrong. But, you cannot be his dumping ground. You cannot be the trash can for him. You can no longer be a place where he deposits his life's frustrations and pains, then leaves, expects you to take out his trash, and goes back to sleep peacefully next to his wife.

HEALING JOURNEY | Day Six

More thoughts and lessons: I let him hunt me because I was curious, thirsty and hungry. I was selfish in my emotional needs. I had unrealistic expectations for someone who only wanted to fulfill fantasies and a bucket list item. I expected for him to tell me the truth, show regard and concern, give me attention—when he wasn't even doing that for his wife.

HEALING JOURNEY | Day Seven

All in one day I was hit with "Memory Lane Bombs." His song came on the radio, I saw his favorite color, and I came across a picture in my photo gallery. Gosh, I miss him so much.

I wanted to believe in him. I wanted to believe that he was actually a good man but he's not in certain areas. He's a cheater. Ughh! Damn character flaws!

HEALING JOURNEY | Day Eight

In the midst of my sexual experiences and escapades with him and with myself, I still got up and went to my closet to pray. I prayed, made declarations over my life and prayed in my heavenly language with a lowly heart. I asked God for this man to reject me before we became intimately involved. I wanted Him (God) to stop the relationship—but it didn't happen this time—not like the other ones. Why?

· · ·

HEALING JOURNEY | **Day Nine**

Late in the evening, early in the morning, midday and just the entire day...I am going through emotional ties withdrawals; my mind is rehearsing all types of scenarios. I am curled up in a ball, fetal position and sweating it out. I am frozen in time; suspended animation—traveling around this tree, trying to make sense of why he didn't come for me, fight for me or truly care for me when I stopped speaking to him for about one month. I should not have doubled back to rekindle our lines of communication.

HEALING JOURNEY | **Day Ten**

He tricked me. He got me to believe and accept the imperfect and he rested in that he didn't try to make it better or comfortable for me. He asked me to let him "be" and not talk about his other life. He never truly reciprocated my requests and my need for him to share his presence with me more than on his terms. I got played.

He is a master manipulator. He is a Mind and Psyche major who loves to master the mind of another person. I got played from the very beginning.

I should not feel ashamed or feel bad, but I do. However, I have to believe that he shall reap each deceptive word that was released from his lips. I am in my feelings for sure. Am I tripping?

HEALING JOURNEY | **Day Eleven**

I love him but he was just passing through. He was a lesson and could have been a thorn—but God healed the wound that I created by allowing him in my life, soul, and depths of vulnerability. I have to stop looking for answers in others and relief in people. God has the answers and the relief. In fact, God has the rest, the comfort and peace I so desperately need and desire.

HEALING JOURNEY | Day Twelve

He was my "split-rock moment"—a disruptor and a moment in time to teach me significance. I am significant but I must not value it based on others' treatment of me. I must walk away from the pain, the hurt, the rejection and the neglect that was created by me marrying him in my "soul-ish" realm.

He was a counterfeit—I held him in my wallet and spent him like he was mine. He will never be mine—he's not equipped. I tell myself: Cry so that I can release him and others from my soul of hurt. Cry to release hurtful darts. Cry to release rejection. Cry to cleanse. It's detox time. I must break free.

He can't be your knight in shining armor. He can't be present for your wants, needs, and calling. He has prior commitments to attend to. He's not healthy. Pray for him and yourself. Move forward and live.

WHAT HAPPENED? Here it is:

- Kandace wanted so much to be in a meaningful relationship. She was desperate and starving for someone who spoke to the very essence of her life. She was weary with dating men who weren't stimulating her emotionally, mentally, and eventually physically.

- Kandace was mad at God because she felt like He had turned His back on her needs and desires—to be wanted, as well as married.
- Being mad at God, made Kandace an open target and vulnerable to get involved with this married man—not caring about the consequences.
- Kandace's experience was slightly similar to a Biblical story entitled, 'The Prodigal Son.' Where she stepped out into the world, exploring and engaging in ungodly behavior—ultimately forgetting about her godly inheritance and character. Kandace enjoyed the temporary pleasures, the blissful moments, and the ethereal atmosphere. However, all these temporary pleasures came to an end. She hit rock bottom, which ultimately made her look up and realize that she was in the wrong place according to her spiritual lineage.
- Kandace's pain in her soul and heart strings for doing the right thing led her back to the bosom of Jesus. This was the only place she could find comfort for her soul.

CAUTION:

If Kandace does not drop her toxic past, she will "leave the door open" for the unhappily married man to come back. He will not even have to knock because she had given him the keys to her heart. Kandace had given him past permissions to enter anytime because he owned her body and soul.

She must be diligent about dropping her toxic past and

healing from the following emotional wounds or she will fall back into this type of relationship with the same guy or with a new guy—who has similar qualities. These emotional wounds would include: (1) Her estranged relationship with God; by asking herself how did she get to the point of being angry with God. (2) Having a mindset that it is ok to have an affair. Asking herself, "Where did that come from? How did I get to this point? Why would I engage in such behavior? Are there deeply rooted vengeful, jealous motives in my heart against married women?" (3) Heal from the self-inflicted pains and wounds of rejection, as well as the darts of rejection from the unhappily married man. (4) Forgive herself for lending out the keys to her heart, soul, and body. She must take back her keys, her heart, soul, and body, and choose to give them to God.

In order for Kandace to successfully drop her toxic past, she must not isolate herself from her godly, spiritually rooted and grounded friends. She must not hide under the shadows of shame and guilt. Embarrassment must be evicted out of her psyche and the door locked to depression. There is a need to be transparent and honest with herself while going through the healing process. She will have to release these pains by verbalizing them—meaning, speaking aloud to a counselor or therapist so that she can embrace her mistakes, forgive herself and take baby steps towards freedom.

Kandace must write out her personal healing goals— with one being Peace-of-mind and the other, Love-of-Self. Peace of Mind will lead her down a path of balance, clear thought and non-impulsive behavior. She will be open to receive daily downloads from God, which is wisdom. Kandace's Love of Self will catapult her into a world of new, tender behaviors and a powerful mindset about an internal relationship and external relationships. It's time for Kandace to build up her self-esteem and self-worth. She's got to return to the truth about who she truly is—a beautiful, spiritual being. Ultimately, others will benefit from this ignited knowledge and her powerful, healthy journey.

Finally, Kandace must drop her toxic past and not continue to play tug-of-war with who she presently is, in her truest identity: Loved by God and Priceless.

8

CONCLUSION: HEALING FROM THE PAST
REJECTION VERSUS ACCEPTANCE

Are you looking at life through Rejection-colored glasses or Acceptance-colored glasses? For years, I saw every aspect of my life and relationships through Rejection-colored glasses which almost derailed my life. It almost caused me to miss out on some amazing people and the awesome purpose for my life.

The goal of this book and the final chapter is to help you get off the Rejection path, as well as drop your past mistakes. I want to strongly encourage you to believe that there is a better version of you waiting to come out and to dominate. I want you to live out your days, on this earth, as a winner and to come out of this Journey of Change as a victorious person. I desire for you to go through this life better than you were—not worse.

I am sharing my unfiltered, authentic heart with you in this final chapter. Read this carefully and carry it with you wherever you travel. Healing from your past is paramount. Releasing past mistakes, issues, trauma, pain, hurt or regret are essential to experiencing a peaceful, productive life. You are never going to truly escape hurt and rejection, however, you can master how you respond to it.

Each day we live, our yesterday becomes our past. What occurred yesterday cannot be changed. It *can* be modified or reenacted perfectly. You can even apologize or remember it, but you cannot get back to what happened in the past. So don't live in regret and slowly kill yourself of stress, anxiety, and the disease of worry. We have to stop holding on to the rope of tug 'o war. This prevents us from moving forward because the past keeps us bound, pulls us back, and convinces us to reopen emotional scars, cuts, bruises, and wounds. Just leave them alone. Let them heal. They Are Gone!

I do not discuss my past as if it is the present situation or as if it is a badge of honor or street "cred." My past toxicity is only shared when I feel in my spirit to release it to someone. I do not continue to resurrect those things that have been cremated and buried. I decided that it was time to be OK with me and stop digging up dead bones. I am a new creature, a brand new individual, a new woman who has many valuable treasures to offer the world. The only places my past can live are in my mind, if I speak about it, and if I allow others to bring it up in a conversation. Therefore, I speak nothing of THE past. My past is not where I choose to reside. It is no longer woven into the fabric of my being. I choose to extend grace and mercy to myself so that I can live a life of peace and happiness.

I like to always reference my focus on this Biblical scripture in *Philippians 3:13* New King James Version (NKJV). Many people have used the apostle Paul's words as a personal mantra; it reads, *"Brethren, I do not count myself to have apprehended; but one thing I do, **forgetting those things which are behind and reaching forward to those things which*** *are ahead,...*" Or even better, this is how it reads in the New Living Translation (NLT), *"No, dear brothers and sisters, I have not achieved it, but I focus on this one thing: **Forgetting the past and looking forward to what lies ahead,...**"* Know this: God wants us free from bondage, slavery, fear, insecurities, hurts, pains and mental anguish. Therefore, push forward through your situation and circumstances.

"Drop your toxic past so that you can experience true love." This is what a wise person wrote in a message to me one day. This statement resonated with me down to the core of my being. A lightbulb came on because the essence of this statement translated to this: God wants us to release our past to Him so that we can experience true love from Him. This experience will open us up to recognize and experience authentic human love on this earth. Then, we can reciprocate that love to other human beings so that the cycle continues. This is why we can never allow our flaws, hurts, or pains to become the guiding force in choosing a mate or close friends. We can get into trouble choosing a mate with warped thinking or Rejection-colored glasses.

For me to experience God's love and earthly, authentic human love, I had to tear down walls, dismiss inner vows, and step out into the world. As I stepped out into the world, I had a strong belief that God would guide and protect me as I became vulnerable and transparent with people. I like to think that God sends people across my path only for either a Simple Walk or a Brief Hike up the mountain or for a Lifetime Journey.

A "Simple Walk" person may be a classmate, who is in need of academic assistance. A "Brief Hike" person may be a friend who is in need of assistance with planning or hosting an event. A "Lifetime Journey" person is a 'friend for life' who is there for the long haul, during the good times as well as the obstacles, hurdles, trials, and tribulations. When we misplace or "mis-categorize" people in our lives, its effect causes us to get off-track and become emotionally drained or confused. Every cute guy or girl, who comes across our path, is not for us to date or develop romantic feelings in our heart. They may be there for us to briefly assist with an assignment and then move on. **Here's a tip:**

Evaluate and ask yourself why this person entered your life or crossed your path. Ask yourself one or some of the following questions:

Is this only a business partnership? Is this person here to help me? Am I only to assist them with this one project? Do I only provide this one piece of advice to them? Are they in the wrong category of my life? Did I rush into something by ignoring the initial signs shown by this person? Did I ignore the real reason why they came along? Do I feel good or fulfilled when I am in their presence? Am I happy and uplifted when I leave their presence? These are poignant, serious questions that we must ask ourselves as we are meeting people daily.

There is this cool visual image that I like to use to help me categorize people in my life. It is called the Circle of Life (See graphic below):

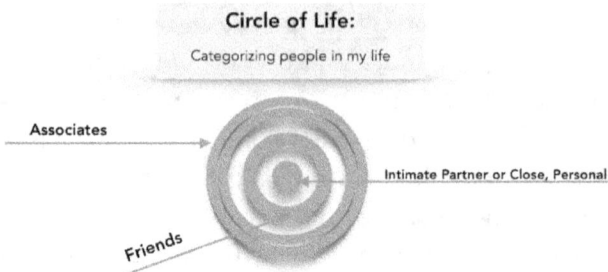

Circle of Life:
Categorizing people in my life

Associates

Intimate Partner or Close, Personal

Friends

The categories are:

- **The Associate Circle** (classmates, family members, neighbors, co-workers, colleagues...) Casual conversations, nothing serious. Communication is on an as-needed basis and/or situational. These people are not privy to my personal business, secrets, flaws or intimate details of my life.
- **The Friendship Circle** (sibling, roommate-friend, best friend, parent, mentor) Spend quality time together, such as shopping or attending an event. Visit each other's home, our families or children play together. Communication is consistent, a little deeper than surface topics. We share highlights of our lives, such as a job promotion, a personal victory, or starting a new business venture. We support each other with our business ventures or event hosting.
- **The Personal Circle** (spouse, someone who keeps my secrets or flaws, no judgment, someone with whom I can be vulnerable and transparent)

Spend considerable, quality time together daily. Someone who knows my deepest, darkest secrets, mistakes, and flaws yet they do not judge or hold them against me. This is someone with whom I can be naked, raw, and vulnerable in any situation. This is someone with whom I can be intimate. *(Intimacy will be with my spouse, of course)* This ring is the smallest of my Circle of Life and only contains me, God, and my spouse or best of the best friend (if there is no marriage).

Please know this: I did not arrive here overnight. My transformation took lots of prayers, daily journaling, spending time alone, a bit of therapy, counseling, lots of coaching, reading, listening to audio and visual self-help messages, but most of all consistency. I had to press forward with some of the action items mentioned on the next few pages.

After changing my mindset, one of the first things I did was stop hiding my life and talents. So, I accepted an invitation, from a close friend, to speak to a small group of women about "How to Heal from Your Past." During my preparation, God placed on my heart to create a timeline of my life from birth to the present. This timeline consists of Birth to the Present occurrences of rejection, acceptance, and triumph. It was powerful! I saw my life on this huge chart paper. There were trends, patterns, bad habits, good habits, and toxic 'roots' that required uprooting, quickly. (See template at the end of this chapter.)

Here is what I did for myself, as well as for countless groups of women over nine years:

- Identified the trauma points and major turning points (positive and negative) in my life by creating the Life's Timeline© reflective activity. (The template is included in the Reference section of this book).
- Observed the behavioral patterns by Identifying the things that could be changed and released the things I could not change.
- Uprooted the roots of rejection by forgiving myself and those who hurt me. I told myself that I must capture and dispel the initial cause of how these rejection wounds became rooted in my life.
- Asked myself if I had made any inner vows and put up walls of protection as a result of rejection-pain.
- Did away with negative inner vows, knocked down walls, and prayed for God's protection as I opened myself up to others, again.
- Daily, I reminded myself that humans get hurt as long as we breathe air. Therefore, I am not alone in carrying this emotion. With authentic support and a positive mindset, I can limit my level and frequency of hurt.
- Revisited Life's Timeline© chart weekly. Evaluated how I currently respond to the hurt and the person who is inflicting the hurt. Remember, we must capture the initial hurt and dispel the attack so that it will not take root as the new norm of my existence. See an example of a fictitious person's timeline of life in the Reference pages.

Now it is time to Drop Your Toxic Past and to begin the

healing process. I have taken the liberty of adding a page filled with life-changing steps that I learned while attending a local Women's Conference mixed with my own experiences and studies. When I jotted down the steps, they literally leaped off the page to make an indelible mark on my heart. I was able to take the steps and change them to fit my personal battles, challenges, and issues I had endured.

Here are the essential steps that I believe one must take in order to reflect and begin healing. Use these steps along with the Life's Timeline© template and the Circle of Life activity, which are included in the Reference and resource pages of this book. Happy Healing!

9

12 STEPS TO CAPTURE AND DISPEL INITIAL ATTACKS OF REJECTION & HURT

***

STEP 1

MAKE A DECISION TO BE A CHAMPION, A
CONQUEROR, AND A WINNER- NOT A VICTIM
OF REJECTION

Research online for Positive Affirmations. Find at least 5
positive declarations that you can say daily about how you
are a winner over Rejection

STEP 2

HAVE AND KEEP A STRONG DESIRE TO BE A VICTORIOUS PERSON IN EVERY AREA OF YOUR LIFE:

If things go wrong on your job, home, or school, please remember that it is not the end of the world. There is a light at the end of the tunnel. Inspire yourself by watching your favorite movie about a character who triumphed over great obstacles.

STEP 3

MAKE YOUR RELATIONSHIP PATHWAY FOCUS SOLELY ON POSITIVITY. EMBRACE POSITIVE CHANGE.

When positive people cross your path, don't hesitate to ask them what makes them so positive, optimistic and/or happy. Learn from them and pledge to use this information as part of your life's approach.

STEP 4

DEEPEN YOUR KNOWLEDGE-BASE ABOUT
HEALTHY RELATIONSHIPS IN EVERY AREA OF
YOUR LIFE:

*Your Job, Home, School, Professional Life, Personal Life, and
Relationships.*
Reading books about how to have healthy relationships,
watching documentaries, studying the life of someone who
succeeded in your area of interest. Also, learn about how to
set boundaries.

STEP 5

SEEK GODLY WISDOM

(If you are a believer in the Word of God) and Positive Mentors and/or Coaches as a mirror to reflect possible inner vows, hinderances and walls in your life. Have these appointed people help you adjust and make the necessary changes in your life. Keep in mind change is not instant. Be patient with yourself.

STEP 6

LEARN-APPLY-LEARN-APPLY TO YOUR LIFE, DAILY. CONSISTENCY IS THE KEY TO SEEING RESULTS.

It may get rough or you may become weary, but do not give up. Get an Accountability Partner who will remain by your side and ensure you reach the finish line.

STEP 7

GUARD THE ENTRANCES INTO YOUR HEART | EYE-GATE, EAR-GATE, MOUTH-GATE.

Blocking Toxicity & Negativity that may try to creep in as a distraction. Set boundaries and keep those boundaries. Boundaries are a healthy way to keep you balanced and stable. Boundaries keep you on the path to accomplishing goals.

STEP 8

PROTECT YOUR HEART AGAINST OLD
THOUGHTS AND PAST TOXIC, DESTRUCTIVE
RELATIONSHIPS.

Memories will try to come back or slowly creep in, but don't
give in to the suggestion. Call your trusted friend or
confidante and verbalize what you are feeling. Get help!

STEP 9

BE SELECTIVE OF WHAT YOU EXPOSE YOURSELF TO; FOR IT MAY BRING BACK UNWANTED MEMORIES

— Music, Movies, Old Shows, Photos, Old gift items, Restaurants, Social Media Followings and Posts

STEP 10

DISASSOCIATE FROM THE PAST AND FORMER GROUPS OF FRIENDS.

Complete the Circle of Life© activity and post it in a place where you can see on a daily basis. Remind yourself about the appropriate categories and boundaries that you have set for yourself.

STEP 11

REMAIN OPEN TO CORRECTION AND BE A TEACHABLE PERSON.

If you trip or fall, don't beat yourself up. Learn from your mistakes. If your Accountability partner or mentor corrects you or *calls you* out on something, don't get upset and stop listening. Listen with wisdom and maturity, reflect and make the change.

STEP 12

GET RID OF YOUR PRIDE AND DEPEND ON GOD (IF YOU ARE A BELIEVER) AND OTHERS FOR SUPPORT AND ACCOUNTABILITY.

It is ok to ask for help. It is ok to change mentors and accountability partners. As you grow and mature, life may take you down a path to forge a relationship with another mentor with different expertise.

WHAT IS YOUR FAVORITE STEP? WHY?

10

MY PRAYER FOR YOU...

I pray that you will begin to accept yourself for how you were divinely created, which includes the gifts, talents, skill set, experiences, unique quirks and idiosyncrasies. I pray that you will see yourself as God sees you. When you look at your reflection in any mirror, glass or pool of water, I hope you are grateful for your face, because it is uniquely created just for you—unless you have an identical twin or a third of triplets.

I pray that you forgive yourself for every mistake you've made; for we all have made mistakes. Cease from beating up yourself, reliving the moment you made the mistake and holding unforgiveness deep in your heart. I pray that you no longer suffer from the torment of your past. I pray that you will finally release regret, negative thoughts, and self-doubt —so that you can live a life of confidence, peace, and ease.

Clarity and wisdom will overtake you like never before and you will begin to make the right decisions. These right decisions will lead you to the right path and the right relationships. Those relationships will flourish and prosper. I make a declaration that as a result of right thinking and right decisions that your body and mind are healed. Your healing will shine like a light and draw others to you for their healing. I declare peace over your life, your family and friends, as well as your purposeful endeavors.

Go forth and be a light! Peace and Blessings to you always.

Your Sister and friend,

RITA MACK

REFERENCE PAGES
RESOURCES: BEGIN TO HEAL

Acceptance Starts Now

The timeline shown below and on the next page are just two examples that I have used personally and during healing workshops.

Example of a fictitious person's Life Timeline

All references are purely fiction and not based on an actual person. Any similarities or similar references are coincidental in nature. Review this sample and then use the blank template to start your timeline.

Name: Rahab Harlotta | Age 37, Female, Single-never married

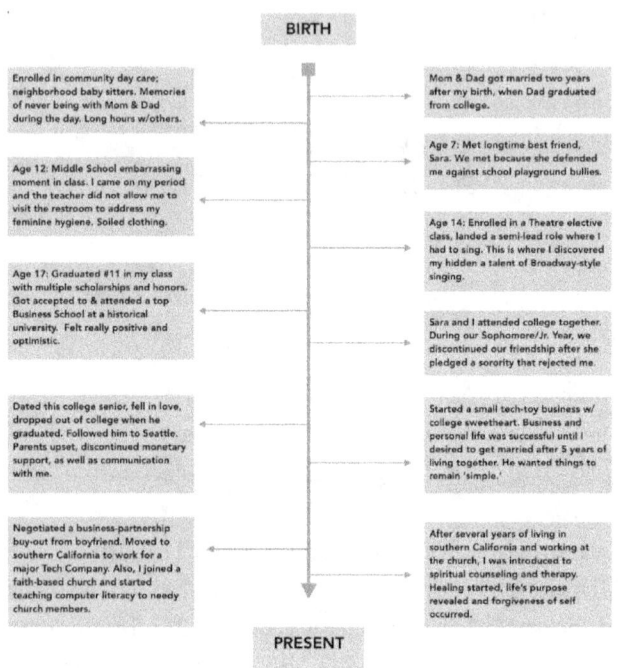

BIRTH

Enrolled in community day care; neighborhood baby sitters. Memories of never being with Mom & Dad during the day. Long hours w/others.

Mom & Dad got married two years after my birth, when Dad graduated from college.

Age 7: Met longtime best friend, Sara. We met because she defended me against school playground bullies.

Age 12: Middle School embarrassing moment in class. I came on my period and the teacher did not allow me to visit the restroom to address my feminine hygiene. Soiled clothing.

Age 14: Enrolled in a Theatre elective class, landed a semi-lead role where I had to sing. This is where I discovered my hidden a talent of Broadway-style singing.

Age 17: Graduated #11 in my class with multiple scholarships and honors. Got accepted to & attended a top Business School at a historical university. Felt really positive and optimistic.

Sara and I attended college together. During our Sophomore/Jr. Year, we discontinued our friendship after she pledged a sorority that rejected me.

Dated this college senior, fell in love, dropped out of college when he graduated. Followed him to Seattle. Parents upset, discontinued monetary support, as well as communication with me.

Started a small tech-toy business w/ college sweetheart. Business and personal life was successful until I desired to get married after 5 years of living together. He wanted things to remain 'simple.'

Negotiated a business-partnership buy-out from boyfriend. Moved to southern California to work for a major Tech Company. Also, I joined a faith-based church and started teaching computer literacy to needy church members.

After several years of living in southern California and working at the church, I was introduced to spiritual counseling and therapy. Healing started, life's purpose revealed and forgiveness of self occurred.

PRESENT

Life's Timeline© Template

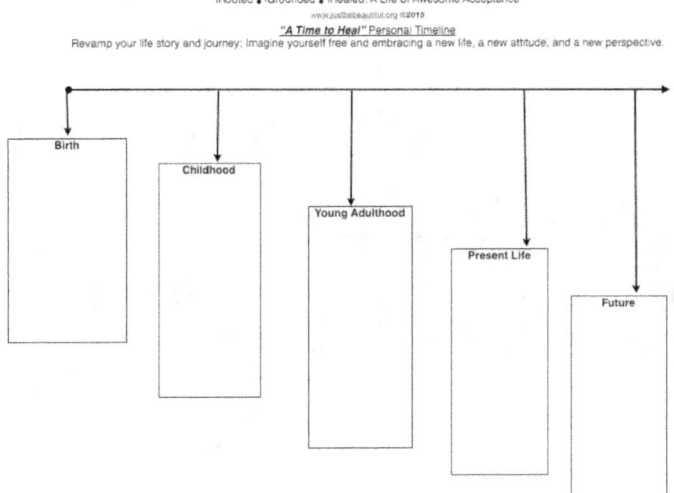

iRooted ∎ iGrounded ∎ iHealed: A Life of Awesome Acceptance
www.justbebeautiful.org ©2018
"A Time to Heal" Personal Timeline
Revamp your life story and journey; Imagine yourself free and embracing a new life, a new attitude, and a new perspective.

Who is in your Circle of Life?

Use this template to map out and identify the people of influence in your life. Then, accurately categorize those people so that you will live a life of peace and balance.

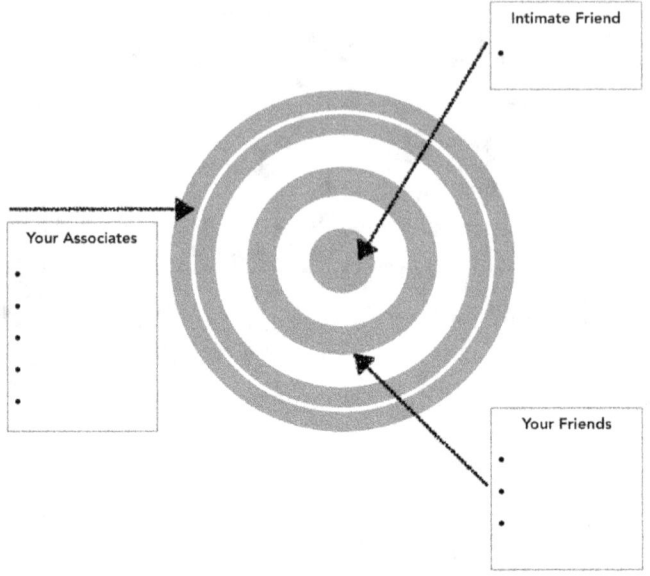

Resource: Child Neglect and Abuse

As a former 22-year veteran teacher, I have had the opportunity to meet, teach, tutor, and mentor hundreds of children and teenagers. During my time as a teacher, I have witnessed unfortunate, disheartening situations in the lives of children and their families. There have been times where I wished that I could care for these kids as my own. I guess that's why I started my girls mentoring organization and published three self-esteem related books for kids and teens. (See Appendix)

I wanted to be more than a bystander. Therefore, I took the liberty of extracting useful resources, shown below, to help others understand, define, and recognize signs and symptoms. Please do not attempt to self-diagnose, moreover, diagnose others based on the information outlined below. I urge you to seek professional help if you recognize these signs or symptoms.

Topic: Child Abuse and Violence
Courtesy of the CDC: Centers for Disease Control and Prevention

Child Maltreatment: Overview
There are four types of child maltreatment: neglect, physical abuse, sexual abuse, and emotional abuse. Each state must develop definitions that meet federal guidelines stated in the Child Abuse Prevention and Treatment Act. Most definitions include the following terminology:

- **Neglect** is failure to provide for a child's basic needs (physical, educational, medical, and emotional).

- **Physical abuse** is physical injury due to punching, beating, kicking, biting, burning, shaking, or otherwise harming a child. Even if the parent or caretaker did not intend to harm the child, such acts are considered abuse when done purposefully.

- **Sexual abuse** includes fondling a child's genitals, incest, penetration, rape, sodomy, indecent exposure, and commercial exploitation through prostitution or the production of pornographic materials.

- **Emotional abuse** is any pattern of behavior that harms a child's emotional development or sense of self-worth. It includes frequent belittling, rejection, threats, and withholding of love and support.

There are three elements in abuse:
1. The Abuser: usually the parent or caretaker
2. The Abused: the child victim
3. A Crisis: a crisis is the precipitating factor that sets the abusive parent in motion.

Definition of a "High Risk Youth": a youth who is less than 21 years old, has been or is, or may be a chemical user and is a:

- *Suicidal tendencies and self-destructive behavior*
- *Abused verbally, emotionally, physically, and sexually*
- *Pregnant and/or sexually active; at-risk for AIDS*
- *Refuses school, truant, drops out, perpetually absent*
- *Emotional problems*
- *Socio-economically deprived*
- *Family of chemical dependents*
- *Involved in occult and practices ritualistic behaviors*

So if any of these aforementioned things occurred in your life, it's time to map out your Life's timeline and seek help from one of the resources below (or similar):

https://www.cdc.gov/violenceprevention/childabuseand neglect/index.html

Childhelp National Child Abuse Hotline:
https://www.childhelp.org/hotline/
1.800.4-A-Child or 1.800.422.4453

Centers for Disease Control: Sexually Transmitted Disease (STDs)

*https://www.cdc.gov/std/products/syndicated.htm

Centers for Disease Control: Provider Pocket Guides, Sexual History

https://www.cdc.gov/std/products/provider-pocket-guides.htm

https://www.cdc.gov/std/products/infographics.htm

National Domestic Violence Hotline: 1-800-799-7233 | 1-800-787-3224 (TTY) or online at https://www.thehotline.org/ OR Text **LOVEIS** to 22522

ACKNOWLEDGEMENTS

There are many thanks and expressions of gratitude that I must share, however, the greatest of these is to my Lord and Savior, Jesus Christ. I am a miracle walking on this earth because of His Grace, Mercy, and Truth.

I am eternally grateful to my Mom, sister, and nephew for investing in the fabric of my life's purpose and mission. This book has manifested into reality because of their support.

A huge THANK-YOU to my first pseudo book editors and proofreaders, who are also my best of friends: Chevette, Angel, Tammy, and Mark. They selflessly allowed me to use them as book taste-testers as I wrote and re-wrote each chapter.

Thank you to my pastors, Creflo and Taffi Dollar for teaching me how to rightfully divide the Word of Truth, as well as apply it to my life with simplicity and understanding. I benefit from their obedience and radical faith-walk.

Thank you to Minister Kevin, Ioyanna, and Siren for

supporting the mission and vision of this book and its positive impact on the organization.

Thank you to Doretha White for being the best book writing coach in the world!

Thank you to Stephan Laboissiere for inspiring our PYP business cohort to write a book, from scratch, with wisdom and courage. The title of this book came about from an interesting discussion I had with someone after completing the PYP business course.

Thank you to my English/Language and Writing teachers from elementary to college, especially, Ms. Barbara Miller. You showed me how to love language, creatively write, and live through poetry.

Thank you to Kia Stephens and Maya Dawson for blazing the book writing trail and allowing me to take a sneak peek along your journey.

Thank you to Suzanne Mohr for the words of wisdom shared as we ministered together in the prisons and detention centers. This experience taught us not to procrastinate and to tell the story while we had the time.

Thank you to my students, mentees, and mentors for believing in the purpose for my life. I am grateful that you entrusted me with your life and time. My experiences teaching and mentoring you all directly impacted my growth and maturity as an author.

Thank you to a host of other precious people who crossed my path and remained in my life or crossed my path and is now gone from my life. I am sure you made an indelible mark on me in some way or another.

Finally, I would like to thank the best editor of all times for not only editing my book with excellence, but for respecting my voice and providing the first 5-star review. Much gratitude to:

CHARELL G. COLEMAN
Editor of Drop Your Toxic Past
Author of The Brown Girl Resilience Book Collection

ABOUT THE AUTHOR
RITA MCGLOTHIN

**Mentor. Teacher. Author. Community Service Advocate.
My Purpose | MENTOR. HEAL. ELEVATE. WIN.**

Rita McGlothin is a graduate of Florida A&M University and Georgia Southern University. She has taught, tutored, and mentored hundreds of young ladies since 1995. Her passion for education, mentorship, and to help children heal from rejection prompted her to create Just Be Beautiful, Inc. Girls Mentoring Organization in 2007.

Rita's mentoring efforts began while teaching in Chicago at the Marva Collins Westside Preparatory School in 1995. She continued to teach and mentor throughout the late 2000's in the state of Georgia. Her academic and mentoring classes have touched the lives of students in grades kindergarten through twelfth. Rita's diligence and consistency caught the eye of leaders and colleagues, causing her organization to be featured in local newspapers and online media outlets. She was also nominated for and won the 2013-2014 Districtwide Teacher of the Year Award for Atlanta Public Schools. Two years later, she was named a 2015 Teacher of the Year Top Ten Finalist for the state of Georgia, as well as a host of other awards and accolades. Rita McGlothin is no stranger to obstacles. She has managed to accomplish many achievements in spite of being partially hearing impaired since the age of five.

Since the incorporation of the mentoring organization, she has impacted the lives of countless girls, women and men with her creative classes, speaking engagements, and community service. Rita continues to host classes and **Toiletry Talk©** sessions virtually, nationally, and locally in Atlanta, Georgia. She also has had the honor of hosting sessions in her hometown, Saginaw, Michigan. Connect with Rita and learn more about her girls mentoring organization here:

www.justbebeautiful.org

@justbebeautiful7

ABOUT THE AUTHOR

Author Rita McGlothin is a successful mentor and founder of a nonprofit Mentoring Organization that specializes in serving the community with puberty and hygiene workshops and resources. She is an award-winning Georgia licensed and certified teacher with over twenty-two years of experience in the public and private education sector. Rita possesses a degree in Ministerial Leadership and Lay Counseling. With a Vegan Health, Nutrition, and Wellness Coach certification, she believes in healing the mind, emotions, and the body in order to live a fruitful life.

RITA MCGLOTHIN

OTHER BOOKS BY THE AUTHOR

Beauty Journal

31 days of positive change for girls & teens

JUSTBEBEAUTIFUL
inside and out.

By Rita L. McGlothin

1st Edition

For more information and to purchase, go to:

www.justbebeautiful.org

DOWNLOADING MY BEAUTY

A GUIDE ON HOW TO THAT SELF-ESTEEM

Volume I

RITA MCGLOTHIN
@justbebeautiful7

For more information and to purchase, go to:

www.justbebeautiful.org

PRETTY. BIG.

IDEAS.

BEAUTY JOURNAL

31 Days of Beautiful Thoughts & Positive Change

BY RITA L. MCGLOTHIN

2ND EDITION

For more information and to purchase, go to: www. justbebeautiful.org